Sanatan

Then, Now, Forever...

Srikanth Polisetti

Published by
PRABHAT PRAKASHAN PVT. LTD.
4/19 Asaf Ali Road,
New Delhi-110 002 (INDIA)
e-mail: prabhatbooks@gmail.com

ISBN 978-93-5562-469-7
SANATAN : Then, Now, Forever...
by Shri Srikanth Polisetti

Edition
First, 2024

Paperback Price
₹ 400.00 (Rupees Four Hundred only)

Printed at
R-Tech Offset Printers, Delhi

Prologue

Hindu scriptures encompass a rich tapestry of spiritual wisdom, rituals, and philosophical teachings. Among the diverse elements found within these scriptures, there exists a particular mantra that venerates the concept of the Chiranjivi, the "immortal beings" or "long-lived ones" in Hindu tradition. This mantra is recited with the intention of invoking good fortune and seeking longevity. The mantra reads as follows:

Ashwatthaama Balirvyaaso Hanumanshcha Vibheeshanaha
Krupaha Parshuramascha Saptaitey Chiranjivinaha
Saptaitaan Samsmareynnityam Markandeymathaashtamam
Jivedvarshshatam Sopi Sarvavyadhivivarjitaha

This chant is a homage to the seven or eight Chiranjivi, considered immortal beings who, according to Hindu belief, continue to exist on Earth across different ages. Each name in the mantra corresponds to one of these revered personalities.

Acknowledgements

First and foremost, I would like to express my deepest gratitude to God for His endless blessings and guidance throughout my life and this journey.

To my parents, whose unwavering support and love have been the foundation of all my endeavours. Your encouragement has been my guiding light and your belief in me has been my greatest strength.

To my beloved wife, Roopa–thank you for your endless patience, understanding, and encouragement. Your love and support have been invaluable throughout this journey. This book would not have been possible without your presence by my side.

With heartfelt thanks,

—Srikanth Polisetti

Contents

Chapter 1

India 1300 B.C. – A Legend is Born

The Present

The relentless patter of raindrops echoes through the somber night. A Maybach manoeuvres its way through the wet streets, finally halting in front of the hospital. An old man steps out, his face etched with worry. With a heavy heart, he enters the hospital, his silhouette disappearing into the gloom. His name is Mohan Mahadev.

Inside, he ascends in the dimly lit elevator. The atmosphere is heavy, saturated with an air of gloom. He arrives at a room and, with apprehension, turns the doorknob. An old lady sits in a corner, her demeanour reflecting the gravity of the situation. She rises and walks towards him.

"How is he?" he asks.

The old woman, wearing a mask of disappointment, nods in response and collapses onto the shoulders of the old man. Together, they share a silent moment of shared grief. He gathers his strength and walks towards the child's bed. The room is hushed, illuminated only by the soft glow of medical equipment. The child, fragile and battered, lies in a hospital bed. His head is shaved, and a network of tubes and pipes sustains his frail body. The atmosphere is laden with the weight of impending loss.

"Have some shame. Chartered flights, political connections, fortune 500 biotech company—all this isn't worth a dime when you can't save your grandson," the old

woman remarks.

"Latha, take some rest, go home. Let me take care of him," he urges.

But the old lady, unable to contain her anguish, pleads desperately. "I beg you. Do what you have to do. But save him. Our family is collapsing."

Overwhelmed, he hugs her tightly, promising solace. "Go home. I will do what is necessary."

Reluctantly, she leaves the room, leaving him alone with his thoughts. He sits on a chair, mechanically picking up a newspaper. The headlines says-"Tragedy befalls on the Mahadev family."

As he absorbs the harsh reality, he gazes into the abyss of uncertainty, determined to do whatever it takes to salvage his family from the brink of collapse.

The old man peacefully dozes off, but suddenly, a noise startles him awake. The nurse is diligently changing saline bottles and attempting to remove the NG tube from his grandson, Omkar. The boy coughs, prompting the old man to rush to his side.

"Don't worry, the pain will go away, Omkar. Just hold my hand."

The nurse deftly puts the NG tube back, and tears stream down Omkar's face.

"Wow, you are a strong boy Omkar." She leaves, and Omkar looks at his grandfather.

"I am in terrible pain..."

"Don't worry, the doctor will give you stronger medicines."

"I don't want medicines... I just want this to end..."

The old man is moved to tears.

"Nothing is going to happen to you."

"Where is dad?"

"He went to get the best doctors for you."

The nurse returns with some food, but Omkar refuses.

"I don't want it..."

"You've got to have food. You will become strong." Says

the old man.

"What's the point of having it when I am anyways going to throw up."

The old man has no answers. He speaks to the nurse.

"Let us give him some time." The old man tells the nurse. She looks sympathetically and leaves them. Observing his grandfather's hands adorned with rudraksha beads, Omkar asks about them.

"What is that?"

The grandfather looks at it.

"Just a reminder that God is with me."

"Is God with me, grandfather?"

"Of course, he is with you. He loves you."

The old man is at a loss for words. He removes the rudraksha and places it on Omkar's bed.

"What happens when God dies? How can he be with everyone if he himself isn't alive?"

"God is immortal, son."

"Then if he loves me so much, why didn't he make me immortal?"

Grandfather is silent, taking a moment to compose himself.

"There are some special humans who are immortal and never die."

Excited, the kid awaits more, but the nurse interrupts, bringing food.

"Please, I don't want to have the food."

"If you have your food, I will tell you an awesome story of an immortal man."

The kid becomes interested, and the old man extends his hand. Omkar hesitates but eventually gives a fist bump. The nurse insists, and Omkar begrudgingly swallows his food.

In the heart of the lush rainforest, a vibrant and untamed world, young Eka opened his eyes to life, welcomed by the rhythms of nature and the whispers of the towering trees. Born into a humble family of hunters, his journey began amidst the enchanting greenery that enveloped their existence. Childhood for Eka was a symphony of playful laughter and the joyful patter of rain on the forest floor, where his companions were not only his family but also the loyal dogs that shared his every adventure.

At the tender age of 8 or 9, the rainforest became Eka's vast playground. The towering trees, the dense undergrowth, and the chorus of exotic birds created the backdrop for his explorations. He developed an inseparable bond with his canine friends, their camaraderie a testament to the interconnectedness of life in the heart of nature.

However, the harmony of his world was shattered one fateful day. The serene ambiance was disrupted by the abrupt snap of a branch. Eka's dogs, keenly attuned to the forest's heartbeat, barked frantically, warning of imminent danger. The boy's innocence transformed into vigilance, and suddenly, a tiger emerged from the shadows, snatching away one of his beloved canine companions. Shock and fear gripped Eka as the majestic predator vanished into the dense foliage.

Tears streamed down his face as grief overcame him, and instinctively, he ran after the fleeting silhouette of the tiger. His mother, a pillar of strength, intercepted him, her voice carrying the weight of concern.

"Stop running behind it... it is gone," she urged, emphasising the irrevocable truth of the forest.

"But my dog...," Eka protested.

"Be thankful that you are alive," his mother reminded him, attempting to impart the harsh yet essential reality of their existence.

"This is my 4th pet that a wretched tiger has taken away...," Eka lamented, his young heart burdened with profound sorrow.

The traumatic incident served as a pivotal moment for Eka. Beyond the confines of family tradition, a deeper calling stirred within him—a determination to become a hunter not merely for sustenance but out of profound love for his loyal canine companions. His father, returning from a hunt with a squirrel in hand, became witness to the burning resolve in his son's eyes.

"Dad, I want to learn hunting," Eka declared, his voice echoing with determination.

"Sure, son... but grow a bit stronger. I will teach you everything I know," his father responded, recognising the fierce determination emanating from the depths of Eka's young soul.

"No, dad, I want to learn now. I have to kill that tiger that keeps taking my dogs," Eka insisted, his passion unfurling like the leaves in the rainforest breeze.

His father, acknowledging the gravity of the request, handed him a bow, instructing him to pull the string. Yet, the young boy struggled, his disappointment palpable as the string eluded his grasp. Understanding the limitations of youth, his father imparted a profound truth.

"You are too young and too weak. I will teach you when the time comes. Meanwhile, you can start with oiling and repairing my bow and arrows. Hunting a tiger is not for the weak-hearted," his father advised, guiding Eka on the arduous path that lay ahead.

And so, amidst the boundless greenery of the rainforest, Eka's journey began—a journey that would sculpt him into a resilient hunter, driven not only by familial duty but by a profound love for the companions who shared his youthful escapades amidst the trees and shadows of the untamed wilderness.

As Eka navigated the challenges of life in the heart of the rainforest, he found solace and strength in a ritual that became an integral part of his daily existence. Whenever he needed blessings or sought guidance for the daunting tasks that lay ahead, Eka would turn to the charcoal drawing of a Shiva Linga on the door of his humble abode.

In the quiet moments of prayer, Eka would gaze upon the symbol of divine strength, hands clasped together in a reverent plea. The Shiva Linga, marked on the door with devotion, became a source of comfort and inspiration for the young hunter-in-the-making. It was more than a mere sketch; it was a conduit to the divine, a connection to forces beyond the realm of the rainforest.

As the years unfolded, so did Eka's journey. The once playful child matured into a skilled young boy, deftly repairing bows and crafting arrows under the guidance of his father. The Shiva Linga on the door became a silent witness to his growth, absorbing the essence of his determination and resilience.

The charcoal drawing, once a simple representation, began to take on additional hues. The strokes of transformation mirrored Eka's evolving spirit—a blend of earthly vigour and spiritual fortitude. The hues painted on the Shiva Linga symbolised not only the passage of time but also the layers of experience, wisdom, and unwavering resolve that Eka accumulated in his pursuit.

The forest, with its challenges and trials, had forged Eka into a resilient young hunter. His connection to the divine, symbolised by the Shiva Linga, fueled his determined spirit to protect those he loved. As the symbol on the door transformed, so did Eka, embodying the harmony of a fierce protector and a spiritual seeker in the heart of the vibrant rainforest.

Eka, the young tribal emerging from the heart of the lush rainforest, embodies the essence of his ancient heritage. With skin bronzed by the sun's gentle caress and adorned in simple yet intricately woven garments crafted from materials found in the forest, Eka carries an air of quiet strength. His eyes, deep and soulful, reflect the wisdom of generations past, while his wiry frame bears the physical resilience honed through a life lived in harmony with the natural world. Eka's hair, unkempt and bearing traces of the earth's richness, dances freely as he moves through the dense foliage, a testament to his untamed spirit.

His mother, a matriarch of the ancient tribal lineage, possesses a grace that stems from years of harmonising with nature's rhythms. Draped in earth-toned fabrics adorned with beads and shells, she exudes an aura of nurturing wisdom. The lines etched on her face tell tales of resilience, and her eyes, warm and discerning, hold the ancient knowledge passed down through generations. A skilled gatherer and caretaker, she moves with a fluidity that mirrors the flowing streams and rustling leaves of the rainforest she calls home.

Eka's father, the patriarch of the tribal family, epitomises the primal connection between man and nature. His physique, weathered by the trials of the forest, emanates strength and stoicism. Draped in animal hides and adorned with symbolic markings, he carries the tools of a hunter and the wisdom of an elder. With eyes that have witnessed the dance of seasons and the eons of tribal traditions, his presence exudes an unwavering connection to the ancient spirits that govern the forest.

Together, as an ancient tribal family from India, Eka, his mother, and his father represent a continuum of life deeply rooted in traditions that have withstood the test of time. Their existence, a harmonious interplay with the rainforest, is a living testament to the enduring spirit of ancient tribal communities in India, where simplicity, respect for nature, and the bonds of family intertwine to form a rich tapestry of cultural heritage.

The guru, despite his humility, found himself constrained by the dictates of state law, rendering him unable to accept Eka as his student. Eka, however, harboured a deep-seated desire to study under the guru's guidance. Undeterred by the unfortunate circumstances, Eka, in a gesture of profound respect, prostrated himself at the guru's feet, seeking his blessings. The guru, recognising Eka's sincerity and understanding the unyielding constraints he faced, offered his heartfelt blessings to the determined young seeker.

With the guru's blessings imprinted in his heart, Eka reluctantly left the gurukul. Despite not being officially accepted as a student, Eka had already embraced the guru as his teacher, a bond forged in the silent exchange of understanding.

As Eka ventured into the forest, he couldn't let go of the profound reverence he held for his guru. Inspired by a symbolic gesture, he collected the very earth upon which the guru had tread, as if preserving the sacred imprints of his mentor's knowledge and footsteps. In a secluded spot, under the sheltering branches of a massive, ancient tree, Eka meticulously fashioned a statue of his guru. Using mud, sand, stone, and wood, he sculpted a representation of the revered teacher who had left an indelible mark on his heart and mind.

This statue stood not only as a physical manifestation of gratitude but also as a testament to Eka's unwavering determination to learn and honour the wisdom of his guru, even in the face of societal restrictions. The forest, now holding the silent witness to this act of devotion, embraced the statue as a symbol of the profound connection between a seeker and his unattainable mentor.

The next day, Eka, fueled by an unwavering determination to learn, concealed himself behind the dense foliage, silently observing the guru as he imparted archery lessons to the princes. Instructing his loyal dog to remain quiet, Eka absorbed every nuance of the teachings. As evening descended, he retreated to a secluded spot to practice what he had gleaned from the day's observations.

In front of the statue he had fashioned in homage to his unattainable guru, Eka initiated a disciplined program of self-study. Every single day, he diligently practiced his archery skills, seeking perfection before the symbolic representation of his revered teacher.

In the initial stages of his practice, Eka's arrows lacked the desired range. However, his perseverance and dedication led him to a serendipitous discovery —an arrow that whizzed past him as he hid beneath the bushes. Intrigued, Eka carefully examined the arrow and set out to replicate it. Combining his resourcefulness, he stumbled upon discarded bows left behind by the princes. With newfound enthusiasm, he crafted a new bow and arrow set, impressing even his hunter father with his ingenuity. Now armed with improved equipment, Eka found himself capable of launching arrows over larger distances.

Over the passing years, Eka's commitment to his craft bore fruit. Through sincere practice and unwavering dedication, he not only learned archery but surpassed the state princes in skill. His proficiency reached such heights that he developed an almost instinctive connection with his surroundings. Hearing the faintest sound of an animal, Eka would swiftly shoot an arrow, claiming his prey with remarkable accuracy.

One day the prince and his entourage ventured into the dense jungle for a hunting expedition, the lush greenery echoed with the sounds of their arrival. Accompanied by a retinue of servants, armed with implements and a pack of dogs, the royal party moved leisurely through the wild expanse. The jungle, with its myriad of sights and sounds, became a backdrop for their pursuit of game.

Among the dogs that accompanied the hunting party, one adventurous canine broke away from the pack, its keen senses leading it deeper into the woods. Unbeknownst to the prince and his entourage, this playful dog stumbled upon Eka, immersed in his solitary archery practice. Eka, adorned with filth from his surroundings, dressed in dark attire, and bearing matted locks atop his head, was a stark contrast to the royal opulence that invaded the tranquility of the jungle.

Startled by the unexpected intrusion, the dog began to bark loudly, disrupting Eka's concentration. Irritated by the disturbance, Eka swiftly grabbed his arrows and skilfully shot them towards the barking dog. The arrows, designed to be non-lethal, served as a warning to the canine intruder.

The dog, unharmed but now adorned with a peculiar construction of arrows around its mouth, hastily retreated from the scene and returned to the prince's camp. The prince and his companions were taken aback as they witnessed the bizarre sight of the dog with an arrow-based muzzle. The ingenious construction, harmless yet effective, prevented the dog from barking. The prince, surprised and intrigued, couldn't help but admire the cleverness displayed by an unseen archer in the heart of the jungle.

Eka's unorthodox method not only protected his practice from unwanted disruptions but also left an indelible mark on the prince's hunting expedition, showcasing a blend of skill, resourcefulness, and the untamed spirit of the jungle.

The prince immediately ordered his servants and soldiers to identify the individual responsible for the dog's arrow-based muzzle.

"Whoever has done this must be a very dangerous man, Your Highness," remarked a nobleman as the search unfolded. Eka continued his archery practice, indifferent to the commotion around him.

Eka continued to focus on his archery, undeterred by the soldiers' hostile approach.

"You uncivilised brute! The prince is coming. Lay down your weapons!" shouted the soldier.

Ignoring the soldier's verbal assault, Eka persisted in shooting arrows with unwavering concentration. As the soldier prepared to resort to force, the prince intervened, ordering him to stand down. With a silent acknowledgment of the prince's authority, Eka bowed respectfully before him.

"Greetings, Your Majesty," Eka spoke, his tone carrying a mixture of humility and determination.

The prince, curious about the origin of the arrows, examined them closely. It didn't take him long to recognise the distinctive arrowheads as his own. Perplexed, he questioned Eka about their source.

"Where did you get these arrows?" the prince inquired.

"Outside the gurukul," Eka responded calmly.

The nobleman, quick to accuse, said, "You have stolen from the prince. You are to be flayed for theft."

"I have not stolen anything. I have merely taken some discarded arrows," he explained, emphasising the distinction.

The prince, sensing an intriguing story behind Eka's actions, took one of the arrows and skillfully shot it towards a distant target. Impressed by the craftsmanship and functionality, the prince shifted his focus to the soldier who had retrieved the arrow-bound dog.

"Did you do this?" the prince inquired, directing his attention back to Eka.

With a simple nod, Eka confirmed his involvement.

"But why?" the prince asked, intrigued by the unusual modification.

"It was disturbing my focus when I was practicing," Eka explained, providing a straightforward rationale for his unconventional solution.

The nobleman, still sceptical, questioned Eka's skill, challenging him to hit moving targets.

"Anyone fool can hit stationary targets. Can you hit moving targets?" the nobleman challenged.

"The dog was moving... When I struck it," replied Eka.

As the tension lingered, the prince, finding amusement in the situation, sought not retribution but a solution. Expressing a desire for better hunting spots, he directed his attention to Eka.

"Are there any good hunting spots here?" the prince inquired, considering Eka's knowledge of the jungle.

Eka, torn between his commitment to practice and the prince's command, responded, "Just beyond the hill."

The prince ordered Eka to lead the way, "take us."

"I must practice," said Eka.

"How dare you refuse the prince. He is not asking you... He is ordering you," shouted the nobleman.

With reluctance in his steps, Eka complied and moved with the hunting party as they ascended the hill. Soldiers flanked the prince, and Eka seamlessly joined their procession. The atmosphere resonated with the subtle sounds of the jungle, enhanced by the melodious chirping of birds in the background.

The nobleman approached the prince with urgency, expressing his concern.

"Dogs naturally bark if they see any strange object or person; that is the nature (dharma) of dogs," explained the nobleman.

The prince listened attentively, intrigued by the nobleman's perspective.

"This boy harmed a dog behaving naturally (exercising dharma). If this dangerous person practices archery, he will cause a lot of chaos in the world by troubling innocent people. He might even attack you someday, Your Majesty," warned the prince.

As the prince absorbed the gravity of the situation, the usual sounds of the jungle were interrupted by a sudden silence. Eka, sensing an impending danger, gestured for silence among the group.

"Be silent; something is wrong," Eka advised.

However, the prince and his friends continued their chit-chat, oblivious to Eka's concern.

"I need wild boar meat for dinner," declared the prince.

Despite Eka's insistence on silence, the group laughed off his request.

"The tribal is asking us to keep quiet," commented one of the prince's friends.

Growing increasingly worried, Eka pleaded with them once again to hush. The prince and his friends dismissed his concerns with laughter. Suddenly, the jungle erupted into chaos as a tiger pounced on the soldiers, creating a frantic commotion. The prince's friends scattered, and even the nobleman ran away in fear. Now face-to-face with the tiger, the prince trembled. A soldier attempted to intervene, but the tiger swatted him away effortlessly. The prince, now in imminent danger, took a shot at point-blank range but missed. Behind him, Eka recognised the familiar tiger that had been stalking his pets.

"Keep calm, don't move; just stay still," Eka advised in a tense moment.

As the tiger approached the prince, its menacing presence sent a shiver down the royal's spine. Unsheathing a blade in a desperate attempt to defend himself, the prince prepared to face the imminent threat. However, just before the tiger could launch an attack, Eka, swift and resolute, released an arrow that struck the tiger's tail with precision.

Eka possessed the skill to end the tiger's life then and there, but he chose not to engage in direct confrontation. The wounded tiger, startled by the unexpected assault, turned and fled into the depths of the jungle. Eka's choice to spare the tiger spoke volumes about his character–a hunter who understood the delicate balance of nature.

The prince, now safe but visibly terrified, stood there, his earlier bravado replaced by the harsh reality of the jungle. Overwhelmed by fear, he involuntarily released himself. The prince, in a state of shock, struggled to comprehend the events that unfolded.

Witnessing the prince's distress, the nobleman took immediate action. Understanding the severity of the situation, he guided the shaken prince away from the scene, leaving Eka alone in the aftermath of the intense encounter between man and beast. The jungle, once again veiled in a blanket of silence, bore witness to the delicate dance between survival and the untamed wild.

As they made their way back through the jungle, the prince's state of shock was palpable. The soldiers carried him with a sense of urgency, while walking alongside, the nobleman overheard the soldiers' conversation.

A soldier who was hefty expressing gratitude for Eka's intervention, remarked, "If not for the tribal boy, the prince would have been dead."

Another soldier who is of shorter stature, seeking clarification, questioned, "The prince didn't kill the tiger?"

"The prince just peed in his pants," the soldier responded, causing an unintended commotion in the group. Annoyed by the soldiers' indiscretion, the nobleman decided to address the situation.

"I will just come in a while, Your Majesty," the nobleman assured, excusing himself momentarily. The prince, still in a state of gratitude, expressed his newfound appreciation, "The boy saved my life. I need him to come to the palace with me."

"Surely, Your Majesty... You need to rest," responded the nobleman, maintaining the decorum around the prince.

Later, the nobleman discreetly took two soldiers and Eka to a secluded corner, away from the prince's hearing.

"I need your help," stated the nobleman.

"What can I do?" inquired Eka.

"I need a specific herb. We have to get back on the mountain," the nobleman explained.

Concerned about his waiting mother, Eka hesitated, "I need to go back home. My mom will be worried."

Emphasising the urgency, the nobleman pleaded, "It is for the prince." Reluctantly, Eka agreed. They embarked on their journey back to the mountain, an air of uncertainty shrouding their path.

At the edge of the cliff, shrouded in the cloak of darkness, Eka diligently searched for the elusive herb, his nimble fingers navigating the rugged terrain. The air was thick with an eerie silence, and the distant rustling of leaves added to the mysterious ambiance.

After a relentless pursuit, Eka's keen eyes finally discerned the distinct outline of the herb he sought. The moonlight filtered through the dense canopy, revealing the plant's delicate form clinging to the rocky surface. Eka cautiously approached, mindful of the precarious edge of the cliff.

With deliberate care, he began plucking the herb, his fingers expertly navigating the leaves and stems. The herbal fragrance permeated the air as he worked, a testament to the potency of the plant. Unbeknownst to him, a shadow lurked in the darkness.

As Eka continued his task, the nobleman, driven by ulterior motives, seized the opportunity. In a treacherous act, he stealthily approached Eka from behind, a dagger clutched tightly in his hand. The night concealed the sinister intentions that lingered in the nobleman's heart.

In a sudden, vicious motion, the nobleman struck. The dagger descended, finding its mark as it pierced Eka's unsuspecting back. A gasp escaped Eka's lips as he crumpled to the ground, the pain searing through his body. The herb-laden hands that had moments ago harvested life now clutched at the wound inflicted by betrayal.

The darkness bore witness to the heinous act, the cliffside echoing with the sinister silence that followed. Eka lay sprawled on the cold ground, his strength waning with each passing moment. The nobleman, callous and indifferent, surveyed the scene, the moonlight casting an ominous glow on the blade stained with the blood of deceit.

Eka's voice trembled with confusion and fear as he found himself confronted by the vengeful nobleman.

"What are you doing?" he questioned, the moonlight casting eerie shadows on his bewildered face.

The nobleman, consumed by anger, unleashed a torrent of accusations. "You bastard, you lowly scum! You have cheated us."

"I didn't do anything wrong. I never harmed anyone," Eka pleaded desperately, his eyes reflecting innocence.

The nobleman, relentless in his condemnation, declared Eka's actions as a crime. Stumbling back, Eka pleaded for his life, struggling to comprehend the severity of the accusations.

"Guru's training was for the prince exclusively, but you cheated and learned everything from afar," the nobleman accused. "You could have killed the tiger, but you didn't. You wanted to make a statement with the prince."

As the realisation of the nobleman's twisted perspective sank in, Eka instinctively moved back, sensing the imminent threat to his life.

"We can't have you alive. You may one day assassinate the prince. Can't trust lowly scum like you. We can't have you teach the skills of the kings to more Shudras like you," the nobleman asserted, trapping Eka in a metaphorical corner.

Desperation and confusion marked Eka's face as he sought some semblance of understanding. "Does the prince know?" he questioned, hoping for a sliver of mercy.

The nobleman callously dismissed the notion. "He would forget scum like you after a good night's sleep." The darkness of the night bore witness to Eka's harrowing fate, entangled in the web of power and betrayal.

In the ominous stillness of the night, the nobleman, consumed by wrath, raised his sword high, ready to strike Eka down. However, Eka's survival instincts kicked in, and with a swift leap, he plunged off the cliff, disappearing into the abyss below. The nobleman, peering into the inky darkness, was met with an eerie silence, unable to discern the bottom of the cliff or the fate that befell Eka.

The nobleman, seemingly satisfied with Eka's disappearance, muttered, "Good riddance," his voice carrying a tone of finality. He turned to the soldiers, a silent warning etched on his face.

"If anyone hears about this, you are dead," he declared, the weight of his authority hanging in the air. The soldiers, under the threat of dire consequences, exchanged furtive glances but remained silent, complicit in the dark secret that now lingered on the edge of the cliff.

As they journeyed back through the dense jungle, the group happened upon the familiar sight of the guru's statue, meticulously crafted by Eka with reverence and dedication. The nobleman, fueled by resentment and anger, abruptly ordered a halt at the sight.

"Burn it," commanded the nobleman.

The soldiers, well-accustomed to unquestioningly following orders, swiftly gathered materials for a makeshift pyre around the sacred statue. Igniting the fire, the flames danced with an ominous glow, enveloping the symbol of Eka's devotion and determination. The crackling and hissing of the burning wood echoed through the jungle, marking the destruction of the embodiment of Eka's aspirations.

The nobleman observed with a grim satisfaction as the flames leapt towards the sky, erasing any trace of the makeshift shrine. The flickering light cast eerie shadows on the surrounding trees, lending a somber ambiance to the unfolding act of destruction.

Once the fire had devoured every fragment of the statue, leaving only a bed of smoldering ash, the nobleman sternly commanded the soldiers to move forward. The remnants of Eka's silent homage now dispersed into the night breeze, carrying with them the echoes of a dream that had been forcefully extinguished.

□

Chapter 2
A Wandering Monk

The Present

The hospital room was filled with a sense of curiosity as Omkar, lying in his bed, eagerly awaited more details from his grandfather's story.

"That's it? That's the story?" Omkar inquired with a hint of disappointment.

A subtle smile played on the old man's lips, and he exchanged a knowing glance with the nurse, who had been quietly listening in.

"The story is just the beginning," the old man replied cryptically, adding an air of intrigue to the unfolding narrative.

Omkar's eyes widened with curiosity, urging his grandfather to continue. The nurse, too, leaned in, captivated by the anticipation of what would come next.

"Let us continue," Omkar urged, his voice filled with excitement. The room seemed to hold its breath, awaiting the next chapter in the tale that promised more than just a simple beginning. The old man, still smiling, began to weave the threads of the story, transporting Omkar and everyone in the room into the enchanting world of his narrative.

Eka lay sprawled on the jungle floor, his body battered and bleeding from the unseen struggle he had endured. Despite his best efforts, he found himself immobilised, the pain surging through every fiber of his being. His faithful pet dog, sensing his distress, rushed to his side and began to lick his wounds in a display of unwavering loyalty.

The air filled with the incessant barking of the concerned dog as it stared into the dense foliage nearby. Something in the bushes had caught its attention, instilling a sense of fear. Eka, trapped in his incapacitated state, could only watch as the dog, now frightened, continued to sound the alarm.

Suddenly, the jungle seemed to come alive with an electrifying presence. A majestic tiger, its coat bearing the patterns of the shadows it emerged from, leaped gracefully into the clearing. It was the very same tiger that had once hunted Eka's pets, and the one Eka had shot but chosen not to kill. The dog recoiled in terror, and the atmosphere intensified with a palpable tension.

The tiger, however, approached Eka with an air of surprising gentleness. It sniffed him, acknowledging the familiar scent, and their eyes locked in a profound connection. In an unexpected turn, the fearsome creature began to lick Eka, its tongue offering a mixture of comfort and gratitude. It was as if the tiger, in its own way, expressed thanks for the mercy Eka had shown earlier.

With a silent nod, the tiger then left the scene, disappearing back into the shadows of the jungle. Eka and his loyal dog were left in the aftermath, the echoes of a unique encounter reverberating through the dense foliage. The jungle, with its enigmatic ways, had woven another chapter into the tapestry of Eka's extraordinary journey.

The night hung heavy in the dense jungle as Eka's parents exchanged worried glances in their humble abode. Eka's absence lingered in the air, casting a shadow of concern.

"It's late. He has never been this late," Eka's mother fretted, her hands anxiously gripping the edge of her worn saree.

"He must have hunted a big game. It must be taking time to get it home," Eka's father tried to reassure her, his voice carrying a hint of concern beneath the attempt at calmness.

Their conversation was abruptly interrupted by the abrupt barking of the dog outside. A sudden tension gripped the atmosphere, and both parents instinctively rushed out to investigate. The faithful dog, usually a companion, now stood in the courtyard, barking persistently at the darkness beyond.

"Lock yourself in. I will come back in a while," Eka's father instructed with a stern yet caring gaze. He swiftly armed himself with a bow and arrow, glancing back at his worried wife before stepping into the mysterious shadows of the jungle.

Before disappearing into the dark embrace of the trees, he paused to offer a silent prayer. His calloused hands touched a charcoal drawing of Lord Shiva on the door, seeking divine protection and guidance.

The dog, sensing an ally in Eka's father, became a guide in the silent night. Together, they delved into the heart of the jungle, following the faint echoes of Eka's presence.

Eka's father, traversing through the dense foliage, stumbled upon the distressing sight of his son lying on the ground, wounded and unable to move. Concern etched his face as he rushed to Eka's side, attempting to provide immediate assistance. However, the severity of Eka's condition became evident when the father realised he couldn't lift his son unaided.

Filled with a mix of worry and determination, Eka's father spoke comforting words to reassure his son. "Nothing is going to happen. You are fine. I will come back with your uncle," he promised, hoping to alleviate Eka's anxiety about the uncertain situation.

Recognising the urgency of the moment, Eka's uncle soon arrived on the scene. Together, they made a swift decision to move Eka to a more suitable location for proper care. With resourcefulness born out of necessity, they crafted a makeshift bed from available materials and gently laid Eka upon it, ensuring some comfort for the injured young man.

In a desperate bid for help, Eka's father and uncle carried him to the gurukul seeking treatment. Their urgency met resistance at the entrance, where they were denied admission. The commotion, however, reached the ears of the guru, who, curious about the disturbance, emerged from the confines of the gurukul to investigate.

Upon seeing Eka's distressed condition, the guru's expression shifted to one of concern. Despite the plea from

Eka's father, the gurukul's authorities remained adamant about not allowing them inside. The father, in a heartfelt appeal, acknowledged the guru as the same revered teacher whom Eka regarded as his own.

"Sire, please help him," implored Eka's father as the guru stepped forward. The guru, recognising Eka's dire state, conducted a quick examination. Eka, writhing in pain, was unable to comply with the guru's request to move.

"Try to move, boy," the guru advised, but Eka's cries revealed the extent of his suffering. His father, attempting to encourage Eka, echoed the guru's request, but the pain proved insurmountable.

Expressing a sombre realisation, the guru conveyed the unfortunate news. "I am sorry; we can't do anything. His spine is broken," he explained, leaving Eka's father devastated. The guru, recognising the severity of the situation, offered a harsh truth—Eka could never lead a normal life.

Desperation gripped Eka's father, who pleaded for an alternative. The guru, with empathy in his eyes, suggested, "If you really love your son, I think you must let him go."

In the face of such heart-wrenching advice, Eka's father, unable to fathom the idea of letting go, sought any possibility for salvation. "How can any father let go of his son...is there anything I can do?" he questioned.

The guru, recognising the depth of a father's anguish, offered a fragile glimmer of hope. "Just pray to God...and hope for a miracle," he said, acknowledging the profound uncertainty that lay ahead for Eka and those who loved him.

The next morning, Eka's parents embarked on a desperate quest for solace and divine intervention, carrying him to a Shiva temple in the hope of finding spiritual healing. As they neared the temple gate, the father humbly implored, "Just for our son...please let us enter." Unfortunately, their pleas were met with callous rejection, leading to the father's unceremonious expulsion from the temple premises.

The *pujari*, the custodian of the sacred space, regarded Eka's mother with disdain as she persistently pleaded for entry. "Please let my son see God," she implored, seeking compassion amid their trials. Unmoved by their desperation, the pujari questioned the circumstances that led to Eka's affliction, adopting an accusatory tone.

"Do you know why this happened to your son?" the *pujari* inquired, placing the burden of guilt on the parents and urging them to introspect. Confused and distraught, Eka's parents grappled with the pujari's harsh judgments. The *pujari* asserted, "Your son is in such a situation because of the sins of you or your husband or maybe even him," sealing their fate with a harsh decree.

"You and your husband must ask yourselves some difficult questions and introspect," he added, adamantly refusing entry, citing the temple's sanctity. The *pujari* closed the gates, leaving Eka's parents in despair.

"Better leave from the place soon. We have a holy saint coming. He would leave if he sees people like you near our temple," warned the *pujari*, dismissing them with finality. The earnest plea for entry fell on deaf ears as they were sternly denied access, prompting Eka's parents to seek solace elsewhere for their son's plight.

In a poignant display of faith and desperation, Eka's parents carried him on a makeshift basket–the very same one that Shravan Kumar in the Ramayana used to carry his blind parents. As they traversed the path, each step weighed down by sorrow, they eventually halted near the ashes of the guru.

Eka, overwhelmed with emotion, wept, and his mother, unable to bear the agony, implored him, "Please do not cry. We will take care of you." Seeking solace, she picked up some ashes and, with a mix of despair and anger, threw them on her husband's face. Her tears turned to rage, and she began striking him.

"That so-called holy man says our kid has committed sins... How can a young boy commit sins? You call yourself a Shiva bhakt... Where is your God now? They wouldn't even let us enter the temple... Where is your God when we need him?" she cried out, her anguish echoing through the sacred space.

Her husband, devastated and at a loss for words, attempted to console her, but she pushed him back into the ashes of the guru statue Eka had crafted. Dad, now in tears, questioned, "What can I do?"

"You can start by telling me where is your Shiva... Is he a lie? Does he even exist? How can he make our son suffer like this?" she demanded, her voice a blend of desperation and anger.

With a heavy heart, the father admitted, "I am sorry... I don't know what to say." As he rose from the ashes, a profound discovery awaited him–a black rock in the form of a lingam, a sacred symbol of Lord Shiva. Holding the lingam aloft, he spoke with newfound conviction, "Just because Eka is suffering doesn't mean Shiva isn't there."

Placing the lingam on Eka, they carried him back, clinging to the hope that divine intervention would bring solace to their suffering son. Undeterred by skepticism and the challenges that surrounded them, Eka's father carefully placed the lingam near the sacred tree, adorned it with the ashes from the guru's statue, and gently laid his weakened son nearby. The devout couple initiated their worship, seeking solace and divine intervention to alleviate Eka's suffering.

Initially, it was just the mother and father, their fervent prayers filling the air. Slowly, the fervor of their devotion attracted the attention of curious neighbours who began to gather around the makeshift shrine. Eka lay there, his strength waning with each passing minute, yet his parents continued their unwavering supplications.

Witnessing the family's dedication, some compassionate neighbours started contributing to the makeshift temple. Small extensions were added, someone carved a miniature representation of Nandi, Lord Shiva's sacred bull, and a small temple bell found its place among the humble surroundings.

However, not everyone was supportive. Critics, skeptical of their makeshift god, voiced their doubts. Random strangers questioned the legitimacy of their worship.

"Is this some witchcraft? Just because you found a stone resembling a lingam doesn't mean it is a god," remarked one skeptic.

Another added, "Why would anyone come here when a bigger lingam is just a mile away? Is this some kind of a scam?"

The couple, distressed by the murmurs of doubt, pressed on with their prayers, finding strength in their unwavering faith despite the skepticism that surrounded them.

Amidst the humble setting of their evening meal, Eka's parents served roti with gruel, a modest offering that represented the extent of their means. The mother, filled with concern, attempted to feed her ailing son. Eka, in a state of profound weakness, resembled a mere spectrte, unable to partake in the nourishment offered.

"Please have some food... You won't get better if you can't have food," implored the father, his plea tinged with both love and desperation. However, Eka lay there, resembling more of a lifeless figure than the vibrant young boy he once was.

As night enveloped the small dwelling, the parents retired to rest, their son lying in the midst of their simple abode. In the dim light, Eka's eyes fell upon a drawing of Lord Shiva adorning the wall, a tribute crafted by his own hands in times when life seemed more promising. A wave of emotion washed over him, and tears welled up in his eyes.

In a soft, murmuring voice, Eka began to chant, "Om Namah Shivaya." The sacred mantra echoed through the modest space, a poignant expression of devotion in the face of adversity. The spiritual resonance filled the room, creating an aura of quiet surrender and unwavering faith despite the seemingly insurmountable challenges that surrounded them.

The rhythmic tap of a gentle knock echoed through the humble dwelling. With a sense of curiosity, Eka's father approached the door, opening it to reveal a saintly figure standing before him. The ascetic, weathered by a life of simplicity, stood there with few possessions, dressed in modest attire, his head veiled, and visible skin marked by numerous boils. Despite his unconventional appearance, the father welcomed him with warmth rather than shooing him away. Standing about 7 feet tall, he was the tallest monk Eka's father had ever seen.

"Yes, sir. How can I help you?" inquired the father, embodying the values of hospitality deeply ingrained in his being.

The saint, a tranquil presence amidst life's hardships, responded, "I need a place to stay for the night."

Without hesitation, the father looked around, gauging the simplicity of their abode. Realising the limitations of their modest dwelling, he made a decision. Turning to his wife, they carried their son outside, making room for the saint.

"I am sorry; we don't have many luxuries. You can sleep inside. We will sleep outside," the father offered with genuine humility.

The saint acknowledged the gesture with a serene smile and entered the dwelling. As Eka observed, he noticed a subtle glow emanating from the *theertha* (water vessel) carried by the saint, a mystical aura that hinted at something beyond the ordinary.

The tranquility of the night was disrupted by a distant chanting that stirred Eka's father from his sleep. With a sense of curiosity, he looked around and discovered a saint fervently worshipping in front of the stone lingam, completely absorbed in meditation. Awe-struck, the father brought his wife to witness the divine presence.

In quiet reverence, the parents observed the saint, and the mother, overwhelmed with devotion, hurriedly went inside to prepare prasad, a simple yet sincere offering, while the saint continued his spiritual practice. As the scent of the sacred food wafted through the air, the saint opened his eyes, and the father approached with a respectful demeanour.

"Sir, you are a holy man. You must go further; there is a bigger temple where you can give your prayers," suggested the father.

The saint, with a serene smile, replied, "*Sthana balame kaani, thana balamu kaadaya*," emphasising that a place possesses immense power due to the prayers, the sincerity behind those prayers, and the presence of God residing there, rather than being attributed solely to the people or the place itself.

"I found this place to be more spiritual than the temple," said the saint.

The mother presented the humble meal, apologising for its simplicity. The saint graciously accepted and began eating. The father, expressing concern for their small place of worship, stated, "This is just a rock I found. Only me and my wife pray here for our son."

"In the initial days of spiritual growth, we need a specific place, time, and an Idol to concentrate on God. Gradually, after a few years of our journey into spirituality, we evolve to a position where we see the Almighty in each and every element of His creation. At that time, you no longer need an Idol or visit a temple," explained the saint.

The saint, having observed the sincere hospitality of Eka's parents, felt compelled to offer his blessings.

"Ahluk, I am happy with the way you took care of me. Let me bless you," the saint expressed, prompting a sense of astonishment in the father.

Dad, bewildered, questioned the saint, "Sir, how did you know my name?" To this, the saint smiled, an enigmatic acknowledgment of his spiritual insight. Touched by the saint's presence, the father fell to the saint's feet.

"Holy monk, I don't seek your blessings for myself, but for my son. His need is greater than mine. Kindly bless him with a long and happy life," the father humbly requested.

The saint shifted his gaze toward Eka, lying on the ground, and inquired, "Is that your son?" Receiving a nod from the father, the saint approached Eka with a solemn demeanour.

"He is injured. He isn't able to move his body. Kindly bless him with a long life and cure him of his illness," the father pleaded, voicing the deepest concern for his ailing son.

The saint, with a compassionate yet solemn expression, replied, "I can't do that. Your son is dying. I don't have the power to give life."

Despite understanding the limitations, the father persisted, "I know, sir, but I just want you to bless him. It will make me feel happy." The request carried the weight of a father's desperate hope for his son's well-being, seeking solace in the divine presence before them.

Eka gazed intently at the saint as he took off his head scarf, revealing a distinctive wound on the saint's forehead—a jewel-shaped diamond mark. The atmosphere seemed to shimmer with an ethereal energy as the saint closed his eyes in profound meditation.

With a voice resonating spiritual authority, the saint began chanting sacred words, their vibrations seeming to harmonise with the universe. As he bent down to bless Eka, an unintended yet divine occurrence unfolded. A small metallic container shaped like a lingam, adorned with a red gemstone, cradled in the saint's hands, held the sacred *theertha*—a divine elixir.

In the midst of the sacred ritual, a few drops of the *theertha*, imbued with the saint's blessings, spilled onto Eka's nose. The drops, charged with the essence of the saint's prayers, trickled gently, finding their way into Eka's open mouth. It was a moment of divine intervention, where the sacred elixir, touched by the saint's spiritual potency, became an unintentional conduit of blessings.

As the final words, "Deerghayushmaan bhava," reverberated through the air, Eka felt a subtle shift within him.

After blessing Eka, the saint prepared to depart.

"Thank you, sir... Sir, will you return?" inquired Dad.

"I will, but not in your lifetime," responded the saint with mysterious certainty.

With those cryptic words resonating in the air, the saint commenced his departure, retracing the path he had taken. The mom, witnessing this unexpected turn of events, couldn't contain her excitement. She noticed Eka stirring and rising, still in a drowsy state. A mix of relief and joy washed over her. Upon hearing the mom's jubilant exclamation, Dad swiftly rushed towards Eka. The sight of his son awakening from what seemed like a dire state filled him with immense relief and gratitude. Although still drowsy, Eka managed to rise with the help of his father. In that moment of familial joy, Dad turned towards the spot where the saint had stood just moments ago. To his astonishment, the saint had vanished, leaving no trace of his ephemeral presence. The mysterious disappearance added an enigmatic layer to the encounter, fueling the family's belief in the saint's divine nature. The inexplicable events became a testament to the miraculous intervention, leaving the family in awe of the transcendent forces that had briefly graced their humble dwelling.

□

Chapter 3
The Immortal

The Present

"I don't get it... how did he wake up? What did the saint give him?" said Omakr.

"The saint didn't give him anything. He simply blessed him with a long life, and some Amrut from his container fell into Eka's mouth. It's fate," said Old man.

"What is Amrut?" asked Omkar.

"Having Amrut can make a person immortal," said Old man.

"Then why can't you give me Amrut instead of these medicines?" inquired Omkar.

The old man is momentarily caught off guard, unsure how to respond. He glances at the nurse, who seems annoyed, as if to say, "The kid isn't eating because of you."

"You are disturbing my flow. Do you want to know what happened to Eka?" questioned Old man.

Omkar nodded eagerly, intrigued by the mysterious turn of events.

Eka slowly regains consciousness, finding himself standing with his parents. His mother and father embrace him tightly, a mixture of relief and joy evident on their faces.

"Are you alright?" said Dad.

"I have never felt better," replied Eka.

Eka remembers the saint and rushes into the woods but he

couldn't find anyone.

"Who was that?" questioned Eka.

"I have no idea; he is surely a learned man," Dad responded.

"Did he say anything about himself?" inquired Eka.

"No, he did not, but he knew everything about me," Dad explained.

"Will he come back?" wondered Eka.

"He said he will come back but not in my lifetime," replied Dad.

"What does that mean?" Eka asked, leaving Dad clueless.

As they gather for dinner, the atmosphere in the household is one of gratitude and relief. The mother, overcome with happiness, engages in prayer at the Shiv Ling adorning the doorway.

"God himself has saved you. Please don't leave us ever again," she expresses with heartfelt sincerity.

Eka, feeling the urge to explore beyond the confines of home, shares his desire for worldly adventures and the discovery of miracles.

"I want to travel the world and explore other miracles. I can't learn them if I am at home," he conveys to his concerned mother.

She firmly opposes his departure, declaring, "No, you are not leaving us."

Eka, understanding his mother's reluctance, attempts to assure her with a promise, "I promise I will come back in a few years. I wish to find the holy man who has saved me."

His father, more accepting of Eka's aspirations, supports his decision, stating, "Let him go. But Eka, promise you will come back to us."

Eka, sincere in his intentions, promises both his parents before seeking their blessings. As he prepares to depart, his father queries, "Why are you leaving so early?"

"I need to finish some things before I leave," Eka replies, bidding a heartfelt farewell to his family and even taking a moment to say goodbye to his loyal companion, the pet dog.

In the quiet stillness of dawn, Eka, concealed amidst the branches, silently observes the prince undergoing rigorous training. The nobleman, a vigilant presence in the shade, oversees the training session. Sensing an opportunity, Eka deftly retrieves a bow and arrow, positioning himself to witness the prince's archery skills.

As the prince skillfully aims at the bullseye, an arrow mysteriously hits its mark before he releases his own shot. The prince, startled, turns around with the nobleman to investigate, finding no one in sight.

Concerned for the prince's safety, the nobleman commands, "Go check it. The prince is being attacked."

In an unexpected turn of events, an arrow swiftly pierces through the air, finding its mark in the nobleman's eye. The nobleman crumples to the ground in agonising pain, prompting the soldiers to shield the prince. Their vigilant eyes spot Eka perched on the tree.

"It's that tribal boy... Get him!" the nobleman orders, and the soldiers sprint towards Eka. Undeterred, another arrow is unleashed, striking the nobleman once more in the eyes. He falls to the ground, writhing in pain.

Seizing the moment, Eka leaps down from the tree, embarking on a swift escape. The soldiers, disoriented by the sudden turn of events, scramble to pursue Eka as he disappears into the surrounding wilderness.

As the soldiers pursue him relentlessly through the dense woods, Eka weaves through the trees with agility and grace. His initial intent to harm them diminishes, replaced by a mischievous desire for a playful diversion. Taking aim with his bow, he deliberately shoots at their feet, adding an element of humor to the chase. Another soldier feels the sting of an arrow in his rear, causing a mix of frustration and amusement among the pursuing troops.

However, the soldiers' persistence pays off as one catches a fleeting glimpse of Eka dashing through the woods. Responding swiftly, they release a flurry of arrows, one of which finds its mark in Eka's arm.

"Got him... now bring his head," commands the triumphant soldier.

Feeling the pain, Eka doesn't falter. Turning around, he extracts the arrow from his arm, revealing a wound that surprisingly begins to heal rapidly. Confused but determined, he continues his sprint until he reaches the edge of a magnificent waterfall. Hesitating for a moment, fear grips him as he contemplates jumping.

Examining his wounded arm, Eka is astonished to witness the rapid regeneration of the injury. The soldiers close in, surrounding him with a triumphant smirk on their faces.

"Choose between death or the gallows," mocks the soldier, relishing in Eka's predicament.

With little choice, Eka takes a leap of faith, plunging into the water below. The impact is harsh, and his head collides with a submerged stone. THis sight goes blank momentarily as Eka submerges underwater. In the hazy underwater vision, he glimpses a four-legged creature with someone astride it at the riverbed.

"Guy is dead... No way he could have survived," the soldier asserts, unaware of the mystical events unfolding beneath the surface.

Eka battles against the current, swimming with all his might until he reaches the safety of the land. Gasping for breath, he struggles to come ashore, his body battered and bruised. As he crawls onto solid ground, he sees blood and instinctively searches for the wound on his head. To his amazement, the injury, which should have been there, has vanished, leaving behind nothing but unblemished skin.

A smile of disbelief and wonderment plays on Eka's lips. The miraculous healing confounds him, and he looks around to find the mysterious creature he saw underwater. However, to his disappointment, the animal is nowhere to be found, as if it were a fleeting vision from another realm. Eka takes a moment to collect himself, contemplating the inexplicable events that have unfolded, and then, with a renewed sense of purpose, he continues his journey through the woods, leaving the soldiers and the waterfall behind.

□

Chapter 4

A Band of Bandits

The Present

Omkar, curious and engrossed, inquires, "Why did you stop?"

The old man, wearing a gentle smile, responds, "Storytelling is a tough job. My throat is dry. Let me have some water first."

The nurse promptly hands him a bottle, and he takes a few sips to quench his thirst before continuing with the tale.

Eka, quenching his thirst with water in the forest, suddenly finds himself surrounded by a menacing group of bandits. Their leader, known for his ruthless deeds, is none other than Angulimala, infamous for adorning a necklace made of the fingers of the men he has killed.

Angulimala demands, "Who are you, and what are you doing in this deep forest?"

Eka, maintaining composure, responds, "My name is Eka. I am a hunter. I escaped the king's soldiers, and I am roaming in the forest."

Inquisitive, Angulimala probes further, "Why are they after you?"

Eka calmly reveals, "I killed a few of them."

One of the bandits, intrigued by Eka's weaponry, takes his bow and arrow for inspection.

"You made these?" the bandit questions, to which Eka nods affirmatively.

Seemingly impressed, the bandit suggests, "Can you make more arrows like these for us?" Eka, acknowledging the request, nods once again, realising the delicate situation he finds himself in.

The bandits, recognising Eka's proficiency with the bow and arrow, swiftly integrate him into their group. His skills impress them, making him an indispensable member of the gang. In return, Eka shares his knowledge of archery with the bandits, while they teach him the brutal art of brawling. United by a common purpose, they initiate Eka into their ranks by branding him on the neck with a hot poker, marking him with the symbol of their notorious bandit group. However, to Eka's surprise, the brand mysteriously fades away shortly after. Angulimala, the leader, holds Eka in high regard for his exceptional abilities. Under their influence, Eka transforms into a formidable force. The gang engages in looting expeditions, where Eka's deadly accuracy with the bow ensures that escaping targets are rare. He becomes adept at finishing off those who manage to flee using his arrows. As the years pass, Eka immerses himself in the bandit lifestyle, becoming an integral part of their criminal endeavours.

One day, the gang had successfully hunted a deer, and the atmosphere was filled with the savoury aroma of roasted meat. The gang members gathered around, seated on makeshift wooden stools, as Angulimala, the notorious bandit leader, surveyed the scene with a satisfied grin.

The stolen drinks, pilfered from nearby villages, were passed around, and the flickering fire cast a warm glow on the faces of the bandits. The feast was a raucous affair, with laughter, banter, and the clinking of stolen goblets filling the air. Eka, having become an integral part of the gang, participated in the revelry, his eyes reflecting the camaraderie that had developed over the years.

As the gang enjoyed the fruits of their plundered spoils, the sentry recounted the tale of the noon hunt. The deer, a graceful creature of the forest, had fallen victim to the bandits' cunning tactics. Eka listened intently, appreciating the skills of his newfound companions in the art of survival and thievery.

The stolen deer, now expertly cooked over the open flames,

became the centerpiece of the feast. The gang indulged in the rich flavours, savouring their ill-gotten gains while the stolen drinks added an extra layer of merriment to the gathering. They were interrupted by a sentry.

"A saint is walking towards us," said the sentry.

"He won't be having anything valuable," replied Angulimala.

"He is carrying an axe and a bow," reported the sentry.

Eka questioned, "What kind of a saint carries a bow and an axe?"

The sentry suggested, "Maybe it's the king's soldiers, spying on us dressed like a saint."

Angulimala growled, "Eka, Rudra and Vaanara, get me the bow and axe. Find out what his story is. If you have any doubt he is a kingsman, kill him."

They all nod their heads.

The gang of bandits observed the muddy field as the bulky saint walked through, his presence contrasting sharply with the natural surroundings. His robust stature was emphasised by the axe he carried in one hand. The weather turned, and a gentle drizzle began to fall, creating a serene yet ominous atmosphere.

The sentry, keenly observing the approaching figure, expressed skepticism. "Doesn't look like any saint I have seen," he remarked. Eka, always quick to assess potential threats, agreed, "Definitely a spy."

Squinting through the rain, the sentry suggested, "Take a shot, Eka, but don't kill him."

Eka, with a mischievous smile, responded, "Don't worry; he will collapse."

As the raindrops intensified, Eka skillfully aimed and released an arrow. The projectile raced towards the unsuspecting saint. However, in a moment that stunned the onlooking bandits, the sage, without even glancing back, effortlessly caught the arrow with his bare hand.

A collective gasp escaped from the bandits. Undeterred, the sentry urged, "Shoot again." The bandits, their confidence shaken, awaited the unfolding events with a mixture of awe and uncertainty.

Eka, perturbed by the unexpected turn of events, hastily reloads his arrow and takes aim once more. The bulky saint continues to walk away, seemingly unperturbed. Eka releases the arrow, anticipating a hit, but to his shock, the saint effortlessly dodges it, showcasing remarkable agility. This unforeseen twist leaves Eka bewildered; he had never missed a target before.

Reacting swiftly, the bandits charge at the saint, attempting to overpower him. However, the bulky figure proves to be formidable. In a single, powerful stroke with his axe, the saint swiftly incapacitates two assailants. Undeterred, a third bandit lunges at the saint with a knife. Sensing the imminent threat, Eka takes aim with his bow, ready to intervene. Surprisingly, the saint catches the attacking bandit and, in a strategic move, lifts him towards the path of Eka's incoming arrow. The projectile pierces through the assailant's mouth, effectively neutralising the threat.

Amidst the chaos, a man standing alongside Eka watches the scene unfold with a mixture of terror and disbelief. Eka, realising the danger they face, urges him, "Get everyone and come. This man is no saint." Determined and alarmed, Eka rushes towards the saint, ready to confront the mysterious and powerful figure in their midst.

□

Chapter 5

The Warrior Sage

The Present

Omkar, curious and engrossed, inquired, "Is it a demon?"

The old man smiled.

"Is it a ghost?" Omkar asked again.

"Calm down, kid. Let's keep the suspense rolling," the old man replied with a grin.

The kid smiled back.

Eka, his muscles tensed and his focus sharp, moves into a defensive stance as he approaches the saint. With his bow drawn and an arrow poised for release, he issues a warning, "Stop or I will shoot," but the saint remains unmoved, unperturbed by the impending threat.

Amidst this tense standoff, a sudden commotion interrupts the scene, drawing Eka's attention away from the saint. He turns to see Angulimala and his gang of bandits approaching swiftly, their malicious intent evident in their grim expressions.

Before Eka can react, a sudden, searing pain courses through him as he is struck by a spear launched by the saint. The force of the impact sends him hurtling backward, his body colliding forcefully with a nearby tree. The spear lodges deep into the trunk, impaling Eka and leaving him incapacitated and vulnerable.

As Angulimala and his gang close in on Eka, one of the bandits feigns concern, attempting to offer false reassurance, "You will be fine, Eka," though the truth of Eka's dire condition is undeniable.

Despite the bandit's hollow words, it's clear that everyone knew Eka's was life slipping away with each passing moment.

As rain pours down relentlessly, turning the battleground into a muddy quagmire. Angulimala's eyes blaze with fury as he directs his gaze towards the saint, a primal snarl twisting his lips. With a savage cry, he charges forward, his band of ruthless followers close behind him.

The saint, sensing the imminent threat, discards his bow and grasps his axe tightly, adopting a defensive stance in the face of the oncoming onslaught. As Angulimala and his gang converge upon him, the saint becomes a whirlwind of swift, lethal movements.

In the midst of the rain-drenched chaos, a brutal melee ensues. The clang of metal against metal mixes with the squelch of boots sinking into the sodden earth as the combatants grapple fiercely in the mud. The saint wields his axe with deadly precision, cleaving through bodies with relentless force.

In the close quarters of the skirmish, the saint's combat prowess is on full display. The saint is not content to rely solely on his axe. As fallen bandits litter the ground around him, he seizes the opportunity to arm himself with their discarded daggers, the glint of steel flashing in the dim light. In brutal, close-quarters combat, he unleashes a flurry of strikes, each dagger finding its mark with chilling accuracy. He employs swift, precise strikes plunging the dagger it into vulnerable points with surgical accuracy. Powerful kicks send bandits tumbling backward, their bodies sinking into the mire as they struggle to regain their footing.

As the skirmish rages on, the brutality of the fight intensifies. The saint, fueled by a potent mix of adrenaline and determination, resorts to desperate measures to fend off his assailants. With a grim determination, he resorts to gouging out the eyes of his adversaries, leaving them screaming in agony amidst the mud and rain.

Despite the relentless assault from Angulimala and his gang, the saint remains resolute, his resolve unyielding even in the face of overwhelming odds. Each swing of his axe, each thrust of his dagger, is a testament to his unwavering commitment to defend himself against the forces of darkness that threaten to consume him.

Amidst the chaos of the battlefield, Eka's body trembles with a mixture of pain and astonishment as he witnesses his wounds miraculously begin to mend. The bandit by his side stares in disbelief, unable to comprehend the inexplicable sight before him. With a surge of determination fueled by both agony and defiance, Eka grits his teeth and summons all his remaining strength.

With a primal roar that echoes through the tumultuous air, Eka wrenches the spear from his impaled body, his muscles straining against the agony that threatens to overwhelm him. With a Herculean effort, he loads the spear into his bow, channeling every ounce of his remaining strength into the arrow's flight. With a deafening cry of pain and fury, he releases the projectile, his vision blurring with tears as searing agony courses through his body.

The spear hurtles through the tempestuous air, guided by Eka's unwavering resolve, until it finds its mark with a sickening thud. The saint staggers backward, stunned by the unexpected blow, his grip loosening on his axe as it clatters to the ground.

Seizing the opportunity presented by the saint's momentary vulnerability, the remaining bandits surge forward, their faces contorted with bloodlust. But the saint is undeterred, his resolve steeling as he wrenches the spearhead from his flesh and turns it against his assailants with lethal precision. All of them are slaughtered effortlessely.

Meanwhile, Eka discards his bow and seizes a nearby dagger, his heart pounding with adrenaline as he races towards the fray. With a reckless abandon born of desperation, he throws himself into the heart of the battle, his blade flashing in the rain-soaked gloom.

As Angulimala charges at the saint with a frenzied determination, his dagger poised for the kill, the saint braces himself for the impending impact. With lightning speed, Angulimala's blade finds its mark, sinking deep into the saint's hand. Yet, rather than recoiling in pain, the saint's eyes blaze with a fierce resolve as he wrenches the dagger from his flesh.

With a guttural growl, the saint turns to face his attacker, his movements fluid and precise. Angulimala lunges forward with savage ferocity, his strikes aimed at the saint's vulnerable spots, but the saint deftly evades each blow with an otherworldly grace.

Meanwhile, as Eka, driven by desperation and fear, lunges forward with a sword, the saint's attention is momentarily diverted. With lightning reflexes, Eka's blade finds its mark, slicing through the air with deadly accuracy. The saint staggers backward, his breath catching in his throat as pain lances through his body.

But the saint is not one to be easily overpowered. With a roar of defiance, he surges forward, his hands closing around Eka's throat with a vice-like grip. Eka's eyes bulge with panic as he struggles to draw breath, his vision blurring with darkness.

Suddenly, Angulimala leaps from the shadows, his arms encircling the saint in a bear hug from behind. With a mighty heave, the saint wrenches himself free, his muscles straining against the force of Angulimala's grip.

With a primal roar, the saint retrieves his axe, his movements fueled by a potent mix of fury and determination. With each swing, the air sings with the sound of steel meeting shield, as Angulimala's defenses crumble beneath the relentless onslaught.

But the battle is far from over. As more bandits descend upon the scene, their weapons flashing in the rain-soaked gloom, the saint becomes a whirlwind of destruction, his axe cleaving through flesh and bone with savage efficiency.

Amidst the chaos, Angulimala unleashes a desperate arrow, his aim wild and erratic. With a fluid motion, the saint discards his bloodied axe, the heavy thud echoing through the rain-soaked battlefield. In its place, he retrieves his bow, the sleek weapon fitting naturally in his skilled hands. With deadly precision, the saint releases his first arrow, the shaft slicing through the air with a whisper of vengeance. It finds its mark with chilling accuracy, piercing Angulimala's left hand with a sickening thud. Angulimala's eyes widen in agony as he collapses, his hand rendered useless by the searing pain.

But the saint's onslaught does not relent. With a relentless focus, he fires arrow after arrow, each shot finding its mark with unerring accuracy. Angulimala's right hand, once a weapon of cruelty, is now reduced to a bloody mess, his screams of pain lost amidst the din of battle.

Next, the saint targets Angulimala's legs, his arrows finding purchase in the bandit's flesh with ruthless efficiency. Angulimala writhes in agony, his body convulsing with each agonising strike. Yet, despite the torment, he remains motionless, his gaze fixed upon the saint with a mix of defiance and resignation.

"Who are you?" gasps Angulimala, his voice laced with shock and disbelief as he stares up at the hooded figure standing over him.

Without a word, the saint's hand tightens around Angulimala's throat, his grip firm and unyielding. With a swift, decisive motion, he twists Angulimala's neck, a sickening crack echoing through the air as the bandit's body goes limp.

As the saint turns around, his gaze falls upon the retreating figures of the remaining bandits, their forms blurred by the veil of rain. With a calm determination, he notches an arrow onto his bowstring, the polished wood creaking under the strain as he takes aim with unerring precision.

With a swift release, the arrow flies forth like a streak of lightning, its trajectory guided by the saint's unwavering focus. It finds its mark with devastating accuracy, striking down one of the fleeing bandits with lethal efficiency. The fallen figure crumples to the ground, a testament to the saint's unparalleled skill.

Meanwhile, Eka, his heart pounding with fear and exhaustion, seeks refuge amidst the sheltering embrace of a distant tree. His breath comes in ragged gasps as he presses himself against the rough bark, his mind reeling from the horrors he has witnessed.

For the first time in his life, Eka feels the icy fingers of terror clutching at his heart, his senses overwhelmed by the magnitude of the violence unfolding around him. With trembling hands, he wipes the rain from his brow, his thoughts racing as he struggles to comprehend the impossible odds stacked against him.

And then, in an instant that defies belief, an arrow arcs through the air with impossible speed, its parabolic path slicing through the rain-soaked gloom with uncanny accuracy. With a sickening thud, it pierces Eka's skull, sending shards of agony radiating through his consciousness.

As darkness descends upon him, Eka's final sight is of the mighty saint walking away, his wounds miraculously healed as if by divine intervention.

As Eka's consciousness begins to slip away, his vision blurs into a haze of swirling shadows and fragmented images. Through the fog of his fading awareness, he perceives a dark, four-legged creature approaching, its form shrouded in an eerie aura of otherworldly power.

Upon its back rides a figure cloaked in darkness, his presence commanding and ominous. In his hand, he holds a taut rope, its coils gleaming with an ethereal light. Eka's breath catches in his throat as he realises the identity of the mysterious rider—it is Yama, the lord of death, the keeper of souls.

With a sense of inevitability, Eka braces himself for the final embrace of the reaper's rope, resigned to his fate as his life hangs in the balance. But as Yama casts forth his rope, a strange and unexpected phenomenon occurs—the noose refuses to claim Eka's life.

Yama's expression twists in disbelief as the rope recoils, returning to his grasp empty-handed. His eyes widen in astonishment, his brow furrowing in confusion as he struggles to comprehend this unprecedented defiance of his divine authority.

For the first time in eternity, Yama finds himself thwarted, his power rendered impotent in the face of an inexplicable force beyond his control. With a sense of incredulity, he gazes upon Eka, his mind racing with questions that defy easy answers.

"Lucky," Yama murmurs softly, his voice carrying the weight of eons as he gazes upon the unconscious form of Eka. As Yama rides away into the shadows, his figure gradually fading from view.

As evening descends, painting the sky with hues of orange and pink, Eka slowly rouses from his slumber. Blinking against the fading light, he takes a moment to regain his bearings, his mind still foggy from sleep. With a grimace of pain, he reaches up and removes the arrow lodged in his head, the sharp sting a harsh reminder of the violence that surrounds him.

Surveying the scene before him, Eka's heart sinks at the sight of the bloody battlefield stretching out into the dusk. Corpses litter the ground, their lifeless forms stark against the crimson-stained earth. Crows circle overhead, their raucous cries mingling with the guttural snarls of wolves as they feast upon the fallen.

Among the carnage, Eka's gaze falls upon the butchered body of Angulimala, a grim reminder of the savagery that has engulfed them all. Pushing aside his revulsion, he stoops to drink from a nearby stream, the cool water offering a brief respite from the horrors that surround him.

But his moment of peace is shattered by a noise—a cough, followed by the desperate wheezing of a dying bandit. Rushing to his side, Eka offers the man water, his heart heavy with pity for his suffering.

"Who was that sage?" the bandit gasps, his voice tinged with fear and confusion.

"I have no idea. He wasn't human," Eka replies, his own voice betraying a hint of unease at the memory of the enigmatic figure who had wrought such devastation upon them.

As the dying bandit struggles for breath, a distant sound cuts through the air—a horn, followed by the thundering hooves of an approaching army.

"What's that noise?" Eka asks, his senses on high alert as he scans the horizon for signs of danger.

"The king's men... they're coming," the bandit moans, his voice trembling with dread. "Eka, you must run. Don't let them capture you."

As Eka attempts to lift the bandit, a grim realisation sets in—his injuries are too severe, his strength too depleted for any hope of escape. The bandit's pleas for release from the impending doom of capture weigh heavily on Eka's heart, but he knows he cannot grant such a request.

"I am done. I don't want to be captured. Kill me," the sentry pleads, his voice strained with desperation.

"I can't do that," Eka replies, his voice heavy with regret, knowing that to end the man's suffering would be to betray his own principles.

"They know I am Angulimala's man," the bandit continues, his tone resigned as he reveals a tattoo on his hand—a mark of allegiance that now serves as a death sentence.

Eka's eyes fall to his own hand, expecting to find a similar mark, but to his astonishment, there is nothing—no trace of the tattoo that once bound him to Angulimala's cause. In its place, he finds only smooth, unblemished skin—a silent testament to the healing power of time and the choices that have led him to this moment.

With a heavy heart and a steady hand, Eka takes up an arrow, his fingers wrapping around the shaft with a sense of grim determination. In one swift motion, he raises the arrow and fires, the shot ringing out in the stillness of the night as it finds its mark with deadly accuracy.

As he leaves the dying bandit behind, Eka's gaze falls upon Angulimala's ring of fingers, glinting in the moonlight amidst the blood-soaked earth. For a moment, he is tempted to take it—to carry with him a tangible reminder of the legacy he has left behind. But then, with a resolute shake of his head, he casts the ring aside, leaving it to rest amongst the fallen.

□

Chapter 6

Transformation

The Present

Omkar, curious and engrossed, inquired, "So Yama comes when a person is about to die?"

The old man nodded in agreement.

"Then how come I am not able to see Yama?" Omkar asked.

"That is because nothing is going to happen to you," the old man replied with confidence.

Omkar's face fell into a sad expression. "Eka killed his bandit friend because his friend was in pain. Am I right?"

The old man nodded again.

"I am also in a lot of pain. Isn't it better if I die?" Omkar asked, his voice filled with despair.

The old man was shattered by the question. "Hope is being able to see that there is light despite all of the darkness," he quoted gently. "Your father won't let anything happen to you."

After two decades of absence, Eka finally returns home, only to find that time has stood still in his absence. The familiar sights and sounds of his village greet him, but as he scans the landscape, he realises that something is amiss. Where his family's house once stood, there is now only an empty space, the void a stark reminder of the passage of time.

In its place, Eka spots a small temple-like structure—a

makeshift shrine where his father had once worshipped the idol of Shiva. His heart heavy with nostalgia, he approaches the temple, hoping to find solace in the familiar rituals of his childhood.

As he steps closer, he notices a group of people gathered around the shrine, their heads bowed in prayer. Tentatively, Eka approaches a stranger among them, his voice tinged with uncertainty.

"Where is the house of Aahuk?" he asks, his words echoing with a sense of longing.

The man's surprise is evident as he responds, his tone tinged with sympathy. "There was a house here... but it's gone now. The untouchables, they used to live near the temple. But they've been relocated into the jungle."

Eka's heart sinks at the news, his mind reeling with the implications of the displacement he witnesses. Unsure of what to do next, he casts his gaze around the makeshift temple, his eyes falling upon an old Shiva drawing—his own handiwork from years past.

"Why do you care about them?" the stranger demands, suspicion colouring his tone. "Are you an untouchable? If so, leave now... stop corrupting this holy place."

Venturing into the dense jungle, Eka's heart quickens with anticipation as he searches for the familiar hut hidden amidst the foliage. After what feels like an eternity, he finally spots the humble dwelling nestled among the trees—a sanctuary of memories and familial ties.

Approaching the hut, Eka's steps falter as he takes in the sight before him. His father, once a pillar of strength and vitality, now sits hunched in the corner, his figure frail and weathered by the passage of time. He tends to a small fire, the crackling flames casting flickering shadows across the walls of their humble abode.

"Dad, I'm back," Eka calls out.

At the sound of his son's voice, his father turns, eyes widening in disbelief before breaking into a wide smile. With a speed belied by his age, he rises from his seat and crosses the room in a blur of motion, enfolding Eka in a tight embrace that speaks volumes of the years spent apart.

"Where did you go? You've been away for so many years," his father exclaims, his voice tinged with a mixture of joy and concern.

"I promised you I would be back," Eka replies.

As they pull apart, his father's gaze lingers on Eka's face, his eyes searching for traces of the boy he once knew. "Looks like you haven't aged a day or perhaps my eyesight is getting weaker."

Eka reaches into a pouch at his side, withdrawing a handful of jewels that glint in the dim light of the hut. "These are for you, Dad and this is for Mom," he says, as he presents the treasures to his father.

But as he looks around the familiar surroundings, Eka's heart clenches with a pang of sorrow. "Where is Mom?" he asks, his voice barely above a whisper.

His father's expression darkens with grief as he delivers the crushing news. "Mom died some years ago," he says, his voice heavy with sorrow.

Eka's eyes brim with tears. Without hesitation, he wraps his arms around his father once more, finding solace in the embrace of the man who has always been his rock, even in the face of life's cruelest blows.

"I'm sorry, Dad.How did she die?" Eka's voice trembles with sorrow as he seeks answers from his father, his heart heavy with the weight of loss.

His father's movements slow as he stirs the cooking pot, his gaze distant as memories of the past flood his mind. "Word spread about the miracle man who saved a boy from death. People came to believe that our idol cures people," he begins, his voice tinged with bitterness. "Rich men came and kicked us out of the house. They didn't even let us take our belongings. Your mother tried to get back the idol in the night. She believed that idol is the one which brought you to life..."

His voice falters as tears well up in his eyes, the pain of the past still fresh in his heart. "But she lost her life trying to get the idol back... They killed her... for corrupting the holy place with her presence," he finishes, his words choked with grief as he recounts the tragic events.

Eka's fists clench with rage, his entire being consumed by a fiery anger at the injustice inflicted upon his family. With a sudden surge of emotion, he rises to his feet, drawing his sword with a fierce determination.

"Please don't go. I can't lose you also," his father pleads, his voice quivering with fear and desperation.

But Eka's resolve is unyielding, fueled by a burning desire for justice and retribution. "Nothing is going to happen to me," he declares, his voice ringing with defiance. "I will get our idol back. It belongs to us and our people. Who are they to take it?"

With those words, Eka storms out of the hut, his heart ablaze with righteous fury. His sword held high, he sets out into the night, his every step a testament to his unwavering commitment to reclaiming what was stolen from them and avenging the unjust loss of his mother.

As the soft morning light bathes the surroundings, Eka arrives at his destination. His gaze sharpens as he takes in the sight of the guards stationed around the sacred site. Nearby, a young boy kneels in deep prayer before the idol, his devotion unwavering amidst the early hour when few others are present.

With unwavering determination, Eka draws his sword and swiftly charges at the guards, dispatching them with calculated precision. Though two more guards attempt to defend their post, they prove no match for Eka's skill and resolve, quickly falling to his blade.

Amidst the chaos of battle, the boy continues his prayers, seemingly undisturbed by the violence unfolding around him. As Eka approaches, he addresses the boy with a hint of impatience, urging him to leave.

"Kid, prayer time is over. It's time to go home," he commands, but the boy remains steadfast, his eyes closed in serene communion with the divine.

Growing frustrated, Eka attempts to intimidate the boy, brandishing his weapon threateningly. Yet the boy's serene expression remains unchanged, his faith unshaken by the looming danger.

Desperate to complete his mission, Eka reaches for the sacred Shivling, but to his surprise, he finds it immovable, as if anchored to the earth by unseen forces. Straining with all his might, he struggles to lift the idol, but it remains firmly rooted in place, its weight too great for him to bear.

Suddenly, the boy opens his eyes, meeting Eka's gaze with a calm assurance that sends a shiver down his spine. Startled, Eka recoils, his hand instinctively reaching for his weapon as a sense of unease settles over him. But before he can react, the sound of approaching soldiers draws his attention, prompting him to retreat with the old door bearing Shiva's painting clutched tightly in his grasp.

Returning home to his father, "I could only get this," Eka admits, a tinge of disappointment evident in his voice.

"What about the lingam?" his father inquires, curiosity flickering in his eyes.

"I think they have fixed it to something in the ground. I wasn't able to lift it up," Eka explains, a hint of frustration creeping into his tone.

His father chuckles softly, his laughter carrying a wisdom born of experience. "It's not fixed to anything. Maybe only those who are worthy of faith can lift it."

Perplexed, Eka searches his father's eyes for understanding. "What do you mean, Dad?"

"You have changed. You are not the same person who left this house," his father observes, his gaze filled with a mixture of pride and concern. "People change. Their beliefs change. The world changes. But you know what doesn't change?"

Eka meets his father's gaze, sensing the weight of his words.

"Their discrimination against us," his father continues, his voice tinged with resignation. "Now hurry up. We have to leave. The soldiers will come soon. Someday, I will get that idol back."

As they leave their home behind, Eka carries with him a renewed sense of purpose, fuelled by the promise of reclaiming what is rightfully theirs and challenging the injustices that have plagued their lives for far too long.

□

Chapter 7

The Apex Predator

The Present

Omkar, curious and engrossed, inquired, "How big was the lingam?"

"Not very big. It could easily be lifted by a person," replied the old man.

"Why couldn't Eka lift the lingam?" Omkar asked, puzzled.

The old man smiled.

"In the movie Bahubali, the hero lifts a huge lingam," Omkar continued, clearly perplexed.

"Faith moves mountains, doubts create them," the old man replied wisely. "Eka was not the person he once was. He was a changed man, on the verge of becoming an asura."

"And asuras don't have any power over God and his artifacts," the boy concluded thoughtfully.

As they venture deeper into the jungles, Eka and his father carve out a new existence amidst the wilderness. With skilled hands and resourcefulness born of necessity, they construct a humble abode, weaving together branches and leaves to fashion a small thatched hut that serves as their sanctuary in the heart of the forest.

In the beginning, life in the jungle seems to offer a semblance of peace and tranquility for Eka. However, as days turn into weeks and weeks into months, a subtle shift begins to take hold within him. The relentless struggle for survival, coupled with the bitterness that festers within his heart over the injustices they have endured, begins to corrode the goodness that once resided within him.

Driven by a growing sense of resentment and a thirst for retribution against a world that has wronged him, Eka's moral compass begins to waver. No longer content to passively endure their fate, he succumbs to the allure of darkness that lurks within the depths of his soul.

With a calculated cunning, Eka devises a plan to prey upon unsuspecting travelers who dare to venture into the depths of the jungle. Masking his true intentions behind a facade of innocence, he approaches strangers under the guise of seeking assistance, luring them into a false sense of security with his disarming demeanor.

But as soon as they lower their guard, Eka strikes with ruthless efficiency, overpowering his victims with swift and merciless force. With each act of theft and violence, the once gentle-hearted Eka transforms into a ruthless robber, his actions fueled by a twisted sense of vengeance and a desire to claim what he believes is rightfully his in a world that has shown him nothing but cruelty.

"Eka, I don't like the way we are living. Why don't you start hunting again?" his father suggests, a note of desperation creeping into his voice.

"What's better than hunting humans?" Eka retorts, a sinister grin twisting his features as the darkness within him continues to grow. His descent into evil deeds persists unchecked.

One day, Eka stops a passing caravan, intending to seize their goods as he has done before. However, this time, the travelers fight back, forcing Eka to defend himself. In the chaos, he is compelled to take the life of one of the travelers, but the rest manage to escape. Covered in blood, Eka returns home with what little spoils he managed to salvage.

"I have brought some mutton for us and this golden necklace for you," Eka announces, his voice tinged with false cheerfulness as he presents the ill-gotten gains to his father.

His father's reaction is immediate and decisive. With a look of profound disappointment, he tosses aside the offerings. "I don't want it, Eka. You are better than this. Stop hurting people. This is not what I want you to become. Be kind to the world."

Eka's response is filled with bitterness and resentment. "Why should I be kind to the world when the world was not kind to me?" he retorts defiantly, his resolve hardening with each passing moment. Ignoring his father's plea, he picks up the mutton and begins to devour it, heedless of his father's disapproval.

"Eat if you want to, or you will die of starvation," his father warns, his voice heavy with sorrow.

"I won't eat until you have changed," his father declares, his unwavering conviction underscoring his refusal to accept Eka's descent into darkness. With a resigned smile, Eka leaves.

As Eka's notoriety spreads throughout the land, tales of his ruthless exploits strike fear into the hearts of those who dare to cross his path. One fateful day, as he lays in wait for his next victim, a horse-riding soldier unwittingly falls into his trap. However, to Eka's surprise, the soldier's smile sends a shiver down his spine, signalling that he has stumbled into a deadly ambush.

Before he can react, a group of ten men emerges from the shadows of the surrounding woods, their intent clear as they encircle Eka with malicious grins. Undeterred by the odds stacked against him, Eka's own smile widens as he charges headlong into the fray, his sword gleaming in the sunlight as he meets his foes with unwavering determination. In the ensuing chaos, Eka proves himself a formidable opponent, swiftly dispatching two soldiers with lethal precision. However, his triumph is short-lived as a barrage of arrows rains down upon him, piercing his flesh and sending him crashing to the ground in a hail of agony.

"Bastard is dead," one of the soldiers declares triumphantly, believing they have finally vanquished the elusive forest bandit. But even as Eka lies battered and bloodied, his adversaries waste no time in plotting their next move. With greed gleaming in their eyes, they turn their attention to Eka's rumored wealth, convinced that his nearby house holds untold riches waiting to be plundered. With grim determination, they set off towards his home, their minds filled with visions of the spoils that await them.

As Eka's consciousness fades, he finds himself facing a surreal sight amidst the haze of pain and encroaching darkness. Through the mist, he perceives the imposing figure of Yama, the god of death, riding atop a majestic buffalo. Yama throws his lasso at Eka, but it slips, adding to his confusion. Yama regards Eka with a mix of bewilderment and curiosity, his typically confident demeanour showing a hint of uncertainty in the face of the mortal's defiance.

"What are you? One of these days, I am going to take you with me," Yama responds ominously.

As Eka regains consciousness, he is filled with fury. With determined resolve, he pulls the arrows from his wounded flesh, each motion a testament to his refusal to succumb to the forces threatening him. Despite his injuries, he begins the journey back to his home, his steps fueled by a fierce determination to confront whatever challenges await him.

As the soldiers navigate through the dense forest, the stolen gold glimmers in the dappled sunlight, contrasting sharply with the shadows cast by the surrounding trees. Suddenly, they encounter Eka, standing resolute in their path. Covered in blood and wielding a sword with grim determination, he presents a formidable obstacle to their progress.

The soldiers charge towards Eka without hesitation, their weapons drawn and their faces contorted with bewilderment at his resilience. The archers take aim, but the dense foliage and a straight line of soldiers obstructs their shots. Eka engages the soldiers in a brutal melee, his sword slicing through the air with lethal precision as he defends against their relentless attacks.

Despite the odds stacked against him, Eka proves to be a formidable opponent, carving his way through the ranks of the soldiers with relentless ferocity. As the last swordsman falls, the archers seize the opportunity to unleash a barrage of arrows towards Eka.

Struck in the neck and chest by the archers' arrows, Eka remains undeterred. Smiling defiantly, he continues to advance, sending a chill of terror through the hearts of the archers. Sensing their impending demise, they scramble to reload their bows, but Eka swiftly closes the distance between them.

With lightning speed, Eka dispatches one of the archers, his blows raining down upon his hapless victim with unyielding force. As the second archer prepares to fire a final arrow, Eka seizes the bowstring and swiftly redirects the arrow back towards its sender.

With a sickening thud, the arrow finds its mark, and the archer collapses to the ground, his lifeblood staining the forest floor. Gasping for breath, the soldier struggles to comprehend the nature of his assailant's fury.

"What are you?" he manages to gasp, his voice barely audible.

"I am your end," Eka replies, his voice devoid of mercy.

With a final, decisive stomp, Eka extinguishes the soldier's life, leaving his head to sink into the muddy forest floor. Then, without hesitation, he begins to collect the fallen gold, his senses heightened by the distant plumes of smoke that signal yet another threat on the horizon.

Eka makes his way back to his home, a sense of dread gnaws at his gut when he notices wisps of smoke rising from the direction of his hut. With a sinking heart, he quickens his pace, dropping the stolen gold as he rushes towards the source of the fire. The flames lick hungrily at the thatched roof, casting dancing shadows upon the charred remains of his once humble abode.

Frantically scanning the area, Eka's heart clenches with fear as he spots his father amidst the inferno, his frail form struggling against the onslaught of flames. Ignoring the searing heat, Eka rushes to his father's side, his hands trembling as he helps him to safety.

"Put my ashes in the Ganges," his father rasps, his voice barely audible above the crackling of the flames. "That's where I put your mom's ashes."

"Dad, nothing will happen to you," Eka insists, his voice choked with emotion. "You're fine. Just breathe slowly."

But despite Eka's desperate reassurances, his father's condition worsens with each passing moment. Gasping for breath, he struggles to convey his final wishes.

"I will always be with you," his father manages to whisper, his voice barely audible amidst the roar of the fire. "Please, change for good."

With a heavy heart, Eka watches helplessly as his father takes his last breath, his life slipping away in the flickering glow of the flames. Tears blur Eka's vision as he cradles his father's lifeless form, his cries echoing through the desolation of their destroyed home.

As if to mirror his grief, the heavens open, and rain begins to fall in torrents, mingling with Eka's tears as he mourns the loss of his father. Amidst the devastation, the shiva drawing he had lovingly created lies consumed by the flames, a poignant symbol of the destruction that has befallen their world.

As Eka returns to the scene of the brutal battle, a twisted grin spreads across his bloodied face. With a gleam of madness in his eyes, he kneels beside the fallen soldiers, his hands moving with purpose as he begins to sever their fingers, one by one. With each finger he removes, Eka's laughter grows more sinister, echoing through the silent forest like a chilling omen. As the gruesome task nears completion, he strings the severed fingers together, fashioning a grotesque necklace that hangs heavy around his neck just like Angulimala.

□

Chapter 8

500 B.C – Goutama Buddha

The Present

The child interrupts his grandfather's storytelling, his voice tinged with sorrow and apprehension.

"Please, Grandfather, stop," he implores, his eyes reflecting the weight of the tale.

Curious, the grandfather inquires, "What's troubling you, Omkar?"

"I know what's going to happen next," the child responds somberly.

Undeterred, the old man smiles gently, encouraging the child to continue.

"Tell me, Omkar, what do you think will happen now?"

"Eka will turn into a villain," the child states with a heavy heart.

But the grandfather's expression grows serious as he corrects him, "No, Eka becomes a madman."

Eka, consumed by depression, wanders aimlessly through the jungle, his mind shrouded in grief and anguish. Over time, his despair morphs into seething rage, and he lashes out at anything and anyone who crosses his path. Seeking solace amidst the charred remnants of his former home, he erects a crude tombstone for his father, a solemn tribute to the enduring sorrow that grips his soul.

As the years roll by, whispers of a malevolent presence spread among the locals, instilling fear in those who dare to venture too close to the depths of the jungle. People begin to steer clear of the area where Eka roams, wary of encountering the shadowy figure that haunts its depths. Undeterred by the isolation, Eka retreats further into solitude, sustaining himself by hunting small animals and foraging for fruits and berries.

Then, one fateful day, amid his solitary existence, Eka crosses paths with a saffron-robed monk traversing the wilderness. Driven by instinctual aggression, Eka seizes a hefty branch and embarks on a pursuit, intent on confronting the unsuspecting traveller.

Yet, despite his relentless chase, Eka finds himself thwarted by a baffling phenomenon: though the monk's pace appears leisurely, Eka cannot bridge the distance between them. Frustration mounts with each futile attempt, until exhaustion forces him to confront the enigmatic truth.

Gasping for breath, Eka faces the monk with a mixture of awe and desperation, his voice echoing through the silent expanse of the forest.

Eka implores the monk to cease his movement. "Oh monk, please halt," he requests.

The monk complies, coming to a stop. "I am not moving. I am at rest. It is you who are in perpetual motion," the monk responds calmly.

Finally catching up to the monk, Eka is breathless and exhausted. Unaware that he is speaking to the monk, he demands answers.

"What do you mean by that?" he asks.

The monk explains, "My mind is at rest, while you are yet to find peace of mind." Unmoved by the monk's wisdom, Eka remains fixated on his desires.

"Don't you know who I am? I don't want your wisdom. I want what's in your bag," Eka asserts.

The monk, unperturbed, offers his bag to Eka.

"Take it if that's what makes you happy," he replies serenely.

Eka eagerly snatches the bag, only to find it contains nothing but fruit. Disappointed, he eats one and discards the rest.

"I want your fingers. It will make me happy," growls Eka.

"Which finger do you want?" asks the monk.

Eka's anger reaches a boiling point as frustration and desperation consume him.

"I will take your life. That might make me most happy," he declares vehemently, his voice tinged with desperation and rage.

The monk, unperturbed by Eka's threat, responds with serene acceptance.

"By all means, my child... if it brings you peace of mind," he replies calmly, his words carrying the weight of wisdom and compassion.

Eka is stunned into silence, his anger deflated by the monk's unwavering tranquility. Confusion and remorse wash over him as he grapples with the magnitude of his actions. Tears well up in his eyes as he collapses at the feet of the monk, overwhelmed by a wave of emotions and a profound sense of remorse.

Eka's heart heavy with the weight of his sins, pleads with the monk for redemption.

"Take me with you, oh monk. I have sinned all my life," he implores, his voice trembling with remorse.

The monk, emanating compassion, gently urges Eka to rise.

"Come with me, my son. Let us go," he reassures, extending a hand of solace.

Eka, overcome with gratitude, requests a moment to gather his belongings.

"Give me a minute, master. Let me collect my belongings," he requests, his voice tinged with earnestness.

The monk, understanding Eka's struggle with attachment, offers sage counsel.

"Let go of material comforts, my son. Let go of the past," he advises, his words carrying the weight of timeless wisdom.

"But my father's ashes are in my home," pleads Eka.

"Let go of the past, my son. Death marks the end of this life and the passage into the next," says the monk.

With a solemn nod, Eka relinquishes his earthly possessions, symbolizing his readiness to embrace a new path. He throws away the necklace of fingers.

Led by the monk, Eka embarks on a journey to a monastery, where the monk is warmly received by the disciples. The disciples call the monk Buddha.

"I have brought another brother. Take care of him," says Buddha.

They take Eka in...

□

Chapter 9

400 B.C. – In Search of Nirvana

The Present

The old man gets a call and leaves the kid's side, stepping into a corner to take it. The child watches his grandfather intently as he speaks seriously on the phone. After a moment, the grandfather ends the call and returns to the child.

"Is it Father?" the kid asks.

"Yes," replies the old man.

"Where is he? I want to talk to him," the child cries.

"He's coming. Don't worry. He'll scold you if he finds out you're still not asleep," the old man says.

The kid looks worried. "Should I call him?" he asks again.

"No," the old man says gently. "Let's continue the story."

Eka, now adorned in the simple saffron robes of a monk, has undergone a profound transformation. His once wild and tormented soul now finds solace in the tranquility of his new life. With his head cleanly shaved, he tends to the monastery's lush gardens, nurturing the vibrant flora with tender care. Under the shade of the bodhi tree, he listens intently to the wise teachings of Buddha, each word resonating deeply within his reformed spirit.

Buddha's wisdom echoes through the tranquil air as he imparts profound truths:

"The world is full of sorrow and misery," Buddha teaches, his voice a soothing balm to the troubled soul.

Eka absorbs these words with a newfound clarity,

understanding the root cause of human suffering.

"The cause of all pain and misery is desire," Buddha continues, his words carrying the weight of profound insight.

With each passing day, Eka delves deeper into the teachings, contemplating the nature of desire and its destructive power over the human heart.

"Pain and misery can be ended by killing or controlling desire," Buddha elucidates, his teachings offering a path to liberation from suffering.

Inspired by these teachings, Eka embarks on a journey of inner reflection and self-discipline, seeking to master his own desires and find true peace within.

"Desire can be controlled by following the Eightfold Path," Buddha concludes, his words a beacon of hope for those who seek enlightenment.

Driven by a newfound sense of purpose, Eka devotes himself wholeheartedly to the Eightfold Path, embracing principles of right understanding, thought, speech, action, livelihood, effort, mindfulness, and concentration.

But Eka's transformation extends beyond mere contemplation and study. He finds fulfillment in acts of compassion and service, nursing the sick with gentle hands and cooking nourishing meals for his fellow monks. With humility and grace, he takes to the streets to beg for food, finding joy in the simple act of receiving alms and expressing gratitude to those who offer their generosity.

As Eka wanders the streets, his begging bowl held outstretched in his hands, he encounters a humble abode where a compassionate child offers him a meagre portion of rice. Grateful for the act of kindness, Eka accepts the food with a heart filled with gratitude.

The child, innocence radiating from their eyes, offers Eka more rice, unaware of the turmoil that weighs heavily upon the monk's soul.

"Do you want more rice?" the child asks innocently.

"You are generous, my child. May your mom and dad be blessed," Eka responds, his voice tinged with genuine appreciation.

But the child's response strikes a chord of sorrow within Eka's heart.

"I don't have a father. He was killed by the bandit in the forest," the child confides, his words heavy with the weight of loss.

Eka's heart aches with empathy for the child's plight as he absorbs the gravity of their words. With a heavy heart, he bids the child farewell and begins his journey back to the monastery, his footsteps heavy with the weight of sorrow.

That night, as Eka drifts into uneasy slumber, his mind tormented by haunting visions. In his dreams, he is beset by accusing voices of children, each accusing him of being responsible for the loss of their families. Swept up in a torrent of guilt and despair, Eka awakens with a start, his heart racing with turmoil.

Seeking solace and guidance, Eka returns to the presence of Buddha.

"Why are you looking so sad, my son?" Buddha inquires, his voice gentle yet penetrating.

"Master, my hands are stained with blood. I am a sinner without a future, without hope," Eka confesses, his voice choked with emotion.

But Buddha's response offers a glimmer of hope amidst the darkness that shrouds Eka's soul.

"Repentance is the only fire capable of burning the sins already committed. You are on the right path," Buddha reassures him, his words carrying the weight of wisdom and compassion.

Overwhelmed by the reassurance and guidance of his master, Eka bows his head in reverence.

"Bless me, master. Your presence and words are soothing," he murmurs, finding solace in the profound wisdom and compassion of Buddha's teachings.

As the days turn into weeks and the weeks into months, Eka's presence becomes a beacon of light in the monastery, his kind-hearted nature and unwavering dedication inspiring all who cross his path. With each passing day, he grows closer to attaining the inner peace and enlightenment that Buddha's teachings promise.

□

Chapter 10

Buddham Sharanam Gacchami

The Present

"Where are the fights and action?" screams the kid.

"Patience, Omkar. I promise you, there will be lots of fights and action soon," reassures his grandfather.

Just then, the nurse comes in to check on Omkar, giving the grandfather a weird look before leaving.

Even Buddha was taken aback by Eka's seemingly unchanged appearance over the past ten years. Despite the relentless march of time, Eka remained steadfast in his commitment to walk the path laid out by Buddha.

As Buddha and Eka traverse through the dense jungle, their journey is interrupted by the piercing cries of a woman in distress. Hastening their pace, they soon come upon the source of the commotion: an elderly woman and a young woman lying prone on the forest floor.

"What's the trouble, mother?" inquires Buddha, his voice calm and reassuring.

"My daughter is in labour," the old woman explains, her voice trembling with urgency. "We were on our way to town."

"Can't you ease her pain, master?" Eka interjects, his concern evident in his voice.

"I am dying, help me!" cries out the young woman in anguish.

Sensing the gravity of the situation, Eka looks to Buddha for guidance, his expression a mix of confusion and apprehension.

"Eka, bless the woman and say when I killed people I have killed them out of ignorance. If I speak the truth let the woman get well."

Buddha instructs Eka with unwavering resolve.

"But master," Eka protests, his doubts surfacing, "how can a former ruthless murderer save her?"

With a gentle smile, Buddha remains steadfast in his conviction, urging Eka to trust in the power of his words. Placing his hand upon the woman's head, Eka recites the words imparted by his master, his voice trembling with uncertainty yet infused with a glimmer of hope.

Continuing on their journey, a sense of apprehension lingers in the air as they tread through the dense undergrowth. Suddenly, a faint cry breaks through the silence, followed by the sound of jubilation. Turning back, they witness a miraculous sight: the old woman cradling a newborn baby in her arms. As the cries of the newborn echo through the jungle, the old woman's voice breaks through the stillness, filled with gratitude and relief.

"Sir, you have blessed my daughter and saved her life," she exclaims, her eyes brimming with tears. "Bless my grandson too."

Eka, deferential to his master, suggests, "Let my master bless him."

But the old woman is adamant. "No, I want both of you to bless him," she insists.

Respecting her wishes, both Buddha and Eka bestow their blessings upon the newborn child. With a heartfelt expression of gratitude, the old woman takes her grandson and departs, leaving behind a sense of peace and hope in her wake.

Turning to Eka, Buddha's gaze is gentle yet penetrating, as if searching for the truth within his disciple's soul.

"Eka, are you convinced now that you have overcome your past deeds?" Buddha inquires softly.

"I am, master. Thank you," Eka replies, his voice filled with sincerity and reverence. Overwhelmed with emotion, he falls at Buddha's feet, seeking his blessings.

Buddha, with a gentle touch, offers his blessing, infusing Eka with a sense of strength and purpose.

"Eka, you no longer need me. You must walk alone in the world and spread the word about Buddhism," Buddha instructs solemnly.

"Thank you, master, for saving me. You have given me the strength to go on in life," Eka expresses his gratitude, his heart overflowing with reverence and determination. "Buddham Sharanam Gacchami."

With a final exchange of blessings, Buddha and Eka part ways, each embarking on their own journey, guided by the teachings of compassion, wisdom, and enlightenment.

As Eka embraced his role as a guru, he embarked on a journey that spanned decades, traversing vast territories and spreading the teachings of Buddhism far and wide. For over a century, he roamed from place to place, carrying the light of enlightenment to every corner of India.

During this time, Buddhism experienced a remarkable surge in acceptance and popularity, rapidly gaining momentum like a wildfire across the subcontinent. Supported by the benevolence of Emperor Ashoka, Buddhism transcended borders, extending its influence to Central Asia, West Asia, and even reaching the shores of Sri Lanka.

One of the remarkable features of Buddhism was its inclusive nature. Unlike the rigid caste system of ancient India, Buddhism welcomed people from all walks of life, regardless of caste or gender. Women found a place of equality within the Sangha, the Buddhist monastic community, a stark departure from the societal norms of the time.

The accessibility of Buddhism was another key factor in its widespread appeal. The teachings of the Buddha were conveyed in the simple language of the masses, making them accessible to all. The Buddha's persona, marked by kindness and humility, endeared him to the people, while his profound yet practical philosophy offered moral guidance and solutions to life's challenges.

The patronage of powerful rulers played a crucial role in the propagation of Buddhism. Kings such as Prasenjit, Bimbisara, Ashoka, and Kanishka provided invaluable support, fostering the spread of Buddhism within India and beyond its borders. Emperor Ashoka, in particular, demonstrated his commitment by dispatching his children to Sri Lanka to promote the faith.

Unlike the elaborate rituals of the Vedic religion, Buddhism offered a simpler, more affordable alternative. Its emphasis on ethical conduct, meditation, and mindfulness resonated with people from all walks of life, making it a practical and accessible path to spiritual awakening.

For Eka, the nomadic lifestyle afforded by his immortality allowed him to move freely and spread the teachings of Buddhism without fear of aging or mortality. Buddhism, with its emphasis on non-violence and compassion, provided him with solace and purpose, guiding him away from the pursuit of vengeance against the one who granted him immortality.

Despite his centuries-long journey, Eka found himself grappling with a sense of unfulfillment. While Buddha attained nirvana at the age of 28, Eka, now 900 years old, remained adrift, still seeking enlightenment and spiritual liberation. Yet, his unwavering commitment to the propagation of Buddhism remained steadfast, driving him forward on his quest for truth and salvation.

□

Chapter 11

200 B.C. – The Monk who Gave me Immortality

The Present

"Grandad, can I have a chocolate?" asks Omkar.

"No, you cannot eat such junk," says the old man.

"Please, for the last week, I've been eating only leaves and medicines," the kid requests.

"Your dad would get mad," the old man replies.

The kid looks upset. "Maybe if I had a mom, she would understand," Omkar says, his voice breaking.

The old man feels a pang of guilt. "Okay, tell me what chocolate you want."

The kid's face lights up with a smile.

"And you'd better keep this a secret," the old man warns.

Omkar grins widely.

As Eka continued his travels, his mind preoccupied with the teachings of Buddha and the path he had chosen, an unexpected glint of light caught his eye. Peering across the river, he saw the figure of a saint draped in saffron robes, holding a small metallic container resembling a lingam delicately in his hands. Adorned with a striking red gemstone, the container seemed to emanate a divine glow, casting a mesmerising reflection on Eka's face. The saint was seven feet tall, and there was only one other seven-foot-tall saint Eka had ever seen—the one who had saved his life.

The sight triggered a rush of memories for Eka. It reminded him of the jar of amruth, the elixir of immortality, that he had glimpsed during his childhood. Filled with anticipation, he urged his disciples to steer the boat towards the shore, his heart racing with the hope of reuniting with the mysterious saint.

As they reached the riverbank, Eka's excitement peaked. He called out to the saint, his voice echoing across the tranquil waters, but the figure continued walking away, seemingly indifferent. Undeterred, Eka leaped onto the shore, determined to find the man who had granted him immortality. His disciples, confused by his sudden actions, watched in bewilderment.

However, as he searched the surrounding area, Eka found himself alone, with no sign of the saint or any other living soul nearby.

"What are we looking for, master?" asks one of the disciples.

Eka wanted to explain, but his loyalty to Buddhism prevented him from speaking up. He ventured into a nearby forest in search of the saint, eventually stumbling upon a Shiva temple. Standing before the temple, he faced a dilemma. The vigilant guards questioned his presence, warning him of potential scrutiny.

"Guruji, why are we waiting outside the Shiva temple? We better leave. If someone sees, they might assume we have converted," says one of the guards.

Dejected, Eka returns to the shore, leaving his disciples perplexed and uncertain about their master's intentions.

As the trajectory of Buddhism began to shift, Eka found himself at the centre of its transformation. Despite his best efforts to uphold its values wherever he preached, he encountered numerous obstacles.

Within the Buddhist Sangha, corruption gradually took hold. The allure of valuable gifts led many members astray, tempting them toward lives of luxury and pleasure, disregarding the principles laid down by Buddha.

Buddhism experienced internal divisions, leading to the emergence of various factions like Hinayana, Mahayana, and Vajrayana. The simplicity that characterised Buddhism gave way to complexity and discord.

The adoption of Sanskrit as the language of scripture, particularly during Kanishka's reign at the Fourth Buddhist Council, posed a significant setback to Buddhism's propagation. Sanskrit, comprehensible only to a select few intellectuals, hindered accessibility to the masses and contributed to Buddhism's decline.

Image worship, introduced by Mahayana Buddhists, diverged from Buddhism's fundamental principles, raising doubts about its authenticity and leading to perceptions of assimilation into Hinduism.

Buddhists faced persecution under certain rulers, enduring severe hardships and even death.

Yet, an even greater trial lay ahead—an encounter with an adversary wielding intellect rather than weapons. One hundred years hence, Eka would confront his most formidable challenge within the hallowed walls of his own monastery, before his own disciples.

If only Eka could foresee the profound significance of this stranger's arrival.

□

Chapter 12

700 A.D. – Adi Shakaracharya

The Present

The kid eats his chocolate slowly, relishing each bite. "This is the best thing I've ever eaten in my life," he says with a blissful smile.

The old man, however, is worried. "Finish it fast, before the nurse comes and scolds us both," he urges.

The kid laughs. "You're a billionaire, and you're scared of a nurse?" he teases, laughing even harder.

The old man chuckles too, but their moment is cut short when the kid starts coughing. The old man quickly moves to his side. "That's enough for now," he says gently, taking the chocolate away.

Amidst the serene ambiance of the ancient monastery, a young man sat beneath the sprawling branches of a sacred banyan tree. His presence exuded an aura of impending greatness, his saffron robes billowing gently in the breeze. This was no ordinary figure; this was Adi Shakaracharya, the legendary sage of Hindu history.

Adi Shakaracharya possessed an otherworldly wisdom that transcended his youthful appearance. His eyes sparkled with the light of ancient knowledge, and his countenance radiated a profound sense of tranquility and authority. Clad in saffron robes that seemed to blend seamlessly with the natural surroundings, he embodied the essence of divine wisdom and spiritual enlightenment.

As Eka approached the young sage, he felt a sense of awe wash over him. Here was a being who seemed to embody the very essence of enlightenment, a repository of timeless truths and mystical insights. It was a humbling experience to stand in the presence of such a remarkable individual.

Adi Adi Shakaracharya greeted Eka with a warm smile, his demeanour gracious and welcoming. Despite his youthful appearance, there was a sense of ageless wisdom about him, a depth of knowledge that belied his years. Eka was captivated by the aura of serenity and wisdom that surrounded the young sage, feeling an instant connection to the profound energy emanating from him.

As they exchanged pleasantries, Adi Adi Shakaracharya issued a challenge to Eka—a debate that would test the depths of their intellectual prowess and spiritual understanding.

Despite the warnings and concerns voiced by his followers, Eka embraced the challenge laid forth by Adi Shakaracharya with unwavering determination. To him, this was not just a mere exchange of words, but an opportunity to delve into the depths of existence and ascend to greater spiritual heights.

Driven by a profound thirst for knowledge and a desire to confront the renowned sage who had effortlessly bested Buddhist masters across the land, Eka saw the debate as a chance to test his own understanding and convictions. It was a clash of ideologies and intellects that promised to illuminate the path of truth and reshape the landscape of spiritual discourse.

The terms of their wager added an extra layer of gravity to the proceedings. Should Adi Shakaracharya falter in the debate, he would relinquish his autonomy and become Eka's disciple. Conversely, if Eka were to stumble in his arguments, he would humbly accept Adi Shakaracharya as his master. It was a gamble that held the fate of their spiritual destinies in its balance—a high-stakes exchange that would determine the course of their lives.

Little did Adi Shakaracharya know that he was entering into a profound debate with Eka, a man whose wisdom spanned centuries. Eka, a 900-year-old luminary in his own right, stood ready to challenge the revered sage on equal footing. Thus, amidst the tranquil setting of the ashram, the stage was set for a rigorous debate that would reverberate through the corridors of history, forever reshaping the landscape of spiritual discourse.

Adi Shakaracharya inquires, "How was your day?"

Eka responds, "The question is immaterial and irrelevant."

Perplexed, Adi Shakaracharya seeks clarification, "Oh! Will you kindly state why do you say so?"

Eka explains, "Everything we perceive in the world is illusory and momentary."

Adi Shakaracharya reflects, "So, you're suggesting that the perceived world is transient, an ever-changing illusion devoid of any permanent essence, whether mental or material."

Eka confirms, "Indeed. Everything in the empirical world is but a series of passing dharmas, impersonal and evanescent processes. These dharmas embody the concept of Anatta, bereft of self."

Acknowledging Eka's perspective on momentariness, impermanence, and Anatta, Adi Shakaracharya poses a simple yet profound question, "When you stated 'The question is immaterial and irrelevant,' to whom or what was it immaterial and irrelevant? Who is the subject to whom these perceptions are directed?"

Eka, enraged, retorted, "To no one in particular. There is nothing more to this alleged world's existence than the coordinated flux of a wide variety of elemental, co-dependent factors (dharmas). So, the perception occurred to some non-existent entity."

"Ok! Hypothetically accepting your view, tell me, monk, who is the witness to the arising of dependent elements? Who or what is the witness to the flux? Against what is the flux not static? If you are moving in a chariot at the same speed with another chariot, you will see both chariots as stationary. A perception of speed requires comparison with a stationary object. Likewise, the perception of flux requires a changeless object for a measure of standard. Who or what is that?" asks Adi Shakaracharya.

"I object! What is the necessity of a witness? That too, an eternal permanent witness?! No way such a thing exists. People die and their trace vanishes, things get broken, Worlds get destroyed–all without leaving a trace. Where is permanence?" counters Eka.

"Hold your breath, holy monk. Who is it that sees and says everything is impermanent? That entity has to be present, existent, and permanent," tells Adi Shakaracharya.

"If you say there has to be a witness, who will witness that witness? How would you establish that a witness exists? What you say is wrong because there will be an infinite regress. You say a witness is necessary to claim cognisance. Fine, then tell me, who will say that there is a witness? Where will this infinite loop end? In your theory, everything has to be present to make the witness known," says Eka, taking a sip of water.

"Even if there is any witness, that entity, material or intellectual, will be momentary, ever-changing, always in flux. So, one can't say there is any witness at all," continues Eka.

Adi Shakaracharya responds, "You seem to insinuate that everything is momentary and transitional—the flux keeps on changing every nanosecond, the reality changing every nanosecond just like waves of the sea erase the previous impressions in sand made by the preceding wave. So, who is there who perceives and makes this claim that nothing is permanent? And, against what standard do you measure permanence relative to impermanence? Everything is impermanent relative to what? If everything is temporary, then how would the concept of any sort of permanence even arise? Even to say nothing exists, there has to be a relative plane of existence. Who is the witness, the spectator? There has to be One. The primordial ground, the eternal essence, which is at the basis of everything and from which the whole world has arisen (the Brahman of the Upanishads). There is no void, all that exists is Fullness."

"Come on, then where is the proof that there is something permanent, some ever-present continuum?" says Eka.

"All of us have memories of good experiences, bad ones, many-a-times shared memories. Now let me ask you something, monk. If you say everything is momentary, how do you explain memory? Memory falsifies your entire theory. The [Buddhist] doctrine of momentariness must imply momentariness of the perceiver as well as of the perceived, an implication which the phenomenon of memory proves to be wrong and completely false," replies Adi Shakaracharya.

One of the disciples arrives with some milk.

"Anyways, our milk has arrived. Take this cup in your hand and what do you see?" asks Adi Shakaracharya.

"I see nothing actually. This apparent cup with apparent milk in it, these, at the deepest layer are made up of discrete individual particles. The deepest level of both the material world and our consciousness is considered to be discrete, separate entities. Thus, when we introspect into the deepest layer of our consciousness, we will find that it is composed not from a single homogenous whole but of discrete 'particles'–always in flux, always changing–never permanent," replies Eka.

Adi Shakaracharya smiles.

"Oh, dear friend. I get your point. True there is no real cup–the cup is nothing but made up of clay–clay given another form and shape with heat. So, there is clay inside the cup. The cylindrical object is the mere appearance which we have named a cup, there is no cup as such, but clay in another form. I fully agree when you said you didn't see a cup. But I disagree when you failed to see the clay in the cup. You can never assume clay out. No matter how deep you go, there has to be a smaller and smaller entity which will exist. You cannot extend the hair-splitting to non-existence. In the final split, something has to exist. And it does exist. That is the truth, dear friend. You can't assume that out only because you don't see the subtlest level. You have stopped your quest before you reached the ultimate stage. There is something that is still more subtle and pervades everything. Everything cannot come out of nothing. The deepest truth is single, homogenous, a whole," replies Adi Shakaracharya.

"Oh. What is the proof, Adi Shakaracharya?" asks Eka.

"I can offer you Shruti pramana (scriptures as proof). But you and Tathagat are heretics, you don't believe in the primacy of Shrutis."

"Brahmaivedam amritam
Purastad brahma pascad brahma

Dakshinatas cottarena
Adhas cordhvam ca prasritam
Bahmaivedam visvam idam varishtham.

Translation:

"That Brahman is Eternal.
Brahman in front and Brahman in back,
In the South, on the North,
Also, Overhead and Below—expanded,
This Brahman is the Universe, this is the Greatest."
—Mundaka Upanishad, Mundaka II, Khanda 2, Shloka 12

"The Brahman is known by multifarious names my friend. People perceive it as Atma, Ishwara, Aum—the Pranav, Prjnanam, and there are countless other appellations. Yet, within those names lies nothing but the essence itself.

"I must add, my friend, that your Mahayana Buddhist scripture preaches the existence of the 'Tathagata Garbha' (Buddha-Matrix/ Essence) within all sentient creatures. The notion of Tathagata Garbha is remarkably akin to the Advaitic concept of Atman—the manifestation of Brahman in jeeva. This concept does not differ from a permanent Atman, though you may not accept it! In essence, you embrace the Advaitic view by merely altering the nomenclature!"

Eka, in a fit of frustration, began to storm out of the debate, but Adi Shakaracharya intervened, urging him to stay and finish his milk.

Taking a sip, Eka winced. "By Goutama! It's so hot. My lips are burnt."

"Stop there. What did you just say? Your lips are burnt? You are suffering, aren't you? But at the same time, you say there is no soul. So, who is suffering? Buddha has said that 'there is only suffering, but nobody who suffers.' Is that not a ridiculous proposition? So, for whom are all these teachings? Who were Tathagata's subjects?" questioned Adi Shakaracharya.

Eka retorted, "Come on, Acharya! You too teach about the unreality as the cause of suffering, grief, and pain. The world is nothing but an idea—a dream-like construct where nothing is real. And now why do you criticise our unreality while professing yours?"

Adi Shakaracharya shook his head. "No, you have not understood the true essence of Advaita then. The unreality of the external world that I teach is not based on nothing; it is not nihilist. My concept of unreality does not deny the existence of reality—it is based on flawed perception. Unlike you, I do not assert that there is NO reality at all! I affirm that there is reality, and only ONE reality, but our perception is flawed due to Avidya, Ajnaan, and Maya. Just as the perception of a snake disappears upon realising it is actually a rope on the floor, similarly, upon realising Brahman, one realises that there was never a world of otherness. There was always Brahman, both within and without. You are Brahman. It is an absolute identity, as proved simply by psychological experience. The Shruti maintains '*Tat tvam asi*' (That art Thou); '*Brahmasmi*' (I am Brahman). This is not mere similarity, but full and complete identity – 'I am the Brahman' and 'Brahman is Me.'

"The Great Tathagata perceived suffering, but did not delve deeply into its causes. He recognised the unreality of the workaday world but did not realise the true cause (Avidya) and the entity beyond the cause (Brahman). He did not grasp that strand of argument," concluded Adi Shakaracharya.

"The Tathagata made it clear that he wouldn't delve into the philosophical questions surrounding suffering, focusing instead on the method to end it," declared Eka with a resounding roar.

"I am aware that the Great Buddha steered clear of philosophical and metaphysical inquiries. He did not delve deeply enough. He merely sensed the symptoms of the ailment of suffering, not its true cause. Desires, bondage, and attachment are merely symptoms, not causes. However, the Vedas and the Shruti delved deeper, investigating the source of suffering. Vedanta interprets the Shruti correctly by identifying the real causes as 'Avidya' (nescience) and false imputation (Adhyasa) due to Maya," responded Adi Shakaracharya.

"Acharya!" Eka roared in frustration.

"No, do not say 'Nothing' ever again! The Great Buddhist

teachers did 'exist,' and so did the Tathagata. If you firmly believe in the Tathagata, then you believe in his existence too! Their mortal embodiments were temporary, but their teachings were eternal, their wisdom everlasting. That knowledge is eternal. That's where Brahman shines. It is the light by which everything is seen," exclaimed Adi Shakaracharya with conviction.

Eka, sensing his defeat in the debate, humbly fell at Acharya's feet, pleading, "Master, tell me what I must do."

"It is time for you to return home. Embrace Hinduism and spread its teachings, just as you have spread Buddhism," replied Adi Shakaracharya with gentle authority.

With a bowed head, Eka accepted, saying, "I will do as you say, Guru, but first, allow me to accompany you. Let me embrace Hinduism alongside you."

Adi Shakaracharya nodded in agreement, acknowledging Eka's request.

Adi Shankaracharya's extensive travels spanned the breadth of India, from the southernmost tip of Kerala to the northern reaches of Kashmir, from the western state of Gujarat to the eastern sacred site of Kamakhya. Along his journey, he engaged in profound philosophical debates with scholars from various traditions, including Buddhism, Jainism, and other Hindu sects. Shankaracharya tirelessly preached his Advaita Vedanta philosophy, emphasising the oneness of existence and the ultimate reality of Brahman.

During his travels, Adi Shankaracharya established several *mathas*, or monastic institutions, in strategic locations across the country. These *mathas* served as centers for spiritual learning and dissemination of his teachings, ensuring their continuity and preservation for future generations.

Despite the vast distances he covered, Shankaracharya's commitment to spreading his message remained unwavering. He undertook multiple journeys across India, traversing its diverse landscapes and engaging with people from all walks of life.

Eka marvelled at the realisation that despite his 900 years of existence, he had never embarked on extensive travels across the country, unlike the Acharya. Adi Shankaracharya's profound spiritual journey led him to traverse the length and breadth of India not once, but three times, immersing himself in profound philosophical debates and spiritual exploration. However, this illustrious journey was tragically cut short when Shankaracharya passed away at the tender age of 32 in Kedarnath.

Despite the humility and absence of ego in conceding defeat to Shankaracharya in their debate, Eka underwent a transformative experience. Inspired by the teachings and legacy of Adi Shankaracharya, Eka embraced a new role as a spiritual leader, dedicating himself to the propagation of Hinduism. In his newfound capacity, Eka embarked on a journey to spread the profound wisdom and spiritual insights he had acquired, contributing to the rich tapestry of Hindu philosophy and spirituality.

□

Chapter 13

900 A.D. – Hinduism Homecoming (Ghar Wapsi)

The Present

The nurse shoots an angry glance at Mohan Mahadev.

"What's going on?" Mohan Mahadev inquires.

"Could you step aside for a moment, please?" the nurse requests Mohan.

Mohan complies and moves to the side.

"Is this the appropriate story for children?" questions the nurse.

"What's the harm in sharing the history of our nation?" Mohan responds.

"It's not that discussing our nation's history is wrong, but there's a time and place for everything. Perhaps it would be better to tell him some Panchatantra or Jataka tales," suggests the nurse.

Mohan counters, "Just as there's nothing wrong with showing respect during the national anthem, there's nothing amiss about recounting the illustrious history of our great nation."

The nurse persists, "If you're narrating the history of India to him, he deserves to hear the truth, doesn't he?"

"What falsehood have I spoken? Whatever Adi Shankaracharya conveyed to Eka about particles possibly in flux, where one may not discern what precisely is happening to them... Schrödinger discovered the phenomenon 1,300

years later," Mohan explains.

"I'm not referring to that. Do you honestly believe that Shankaracharya converted all the Buddhists back to Hinduism just through debates? I believe he eradicated them all."

"Even the Buddhists, both past and present, would never assert that! This is a falsehood spread by some who harbour animosity towards Hinduism, unable to accept the fact that Adi Shankaracharya revitalised Hinduism through debates and discussions. Moreover, how could a man with merely four disciples cause harm to Buddhism? There is no historical evidence indicating that Shankaracharya promoted violence or perpetrated killings against Buddhists. Scholars unanimously agree that Shankaracharya was a philosopher and a saint, not a warrior or a king. He was an intellectual who travelled extensively across India engaging in debates to rejuvenate Hinduism, and he passed away at the age of 32. Additionally, Shankaracharya didn't just debate Buddhists; he also engaged with other schools of thought within Hinduism," Mohan explains.

"Then how did Buddhism disappear from India?"

"Buddhism in India faded away due to the incursions of Islamic invaders. Dr. B.R. Ambedkar, in his work The Decline and Fall of Buddhism, has elucidated this fact extensively," Mohan asserts.

"Well, Ambedkar wasn't present when it occurred. I don't agree with him. In the annals of religious history, the proliferation of one religion often begins with the eradication of its opposite counterpart. Hinduism wiped out Buddhism," the nurse argues.

"But consider this: Would Buddhism or Jainism have flourished if they originated in a Christian or Islamic nation, rather than in Bharath?" Mohan questions.

The nurse finds herself at a loss for words, unsure of how to respond to Mohan's statement.

"That's why they say Hinduism isn't just a religion; it's a way of life," Mohan quotes, his voice calm but resolute.

Just then, Omkar calls for his grandfather, breaking the

momentary silence.

"Granddad," Omkar calls out, drawing Mohan's attention.

Turning to face Omkar, Mohan listens attentively.

"What are you guys discussing? Continue the story, please," Omkar requests, his curiosity piqued.

Mohan meets the nurse's gaze and offers a reassuring smile, ready to continue the conversation.

Eka embarks on a journey across Bharat, following in the footsteps of his guru, Adi Shankaracharya, with a group of devoted disciples trailing behind him. As they traverse the diverse landscapes of the land, Eka's gaze falls upon a place that strikes a chord of familiarity deep within him.

In this place, amidst the lush surroundings, stands a magnificent temple, its grandeur echoing the tales of antiquity. The sight triggers a cascade of memories within Eka's mind, transporting him back to a time long gone. It dawns upon him that this is the very spot where his parents sought solace, offering prayers to the sacred lingam when Eka lay injured six centuries ago. Filled with a sense of homecoming, Eka finally arrives at this destination. Welcomed warmly by the temple priests, he is ushered into the sanctum, the same priests who had once denied entry to his father. The irony of the situation does not escape Eka as he reflects on the cyclical nature of existence.

Inside the sanctum, surrounded by the ethereal aura of divinity, Eka performs the rituals with heartfelt devotion before the revered Shiva lingam. Each ritual gesture serves as a portal to his childhood, evoking poignant memories that lay dormant within his soul.

Turning to the temple priest with a sense of curiosity and reverence, Eka seeks to unravel the mysteries veiled within the temple's history.

"Could you enlighten me about the ancient origins of this sacred temple?" Eka inquires, his voice resonating with a blend of reverence and intrigue.

The priest nods in acknowledgment and proceeds to reveal a painting adorning the temple walls depicting a scene from antiquity. In the painting, a valiant prince is depicted hunting a ferocious tiger and rescuing a tribal boy from imminent danger.

According to the priest's narration, on a fateful day, the prince ventured into the forbidden depths of the forest, led astray by the tribal boy. As they traversed the treacherous terrain, they encountered a series of perils, including attacks by bandits and wild beasts, which resulted in the loss of many of the prince's companions. Despite facing mortal danger, the prince bravely intervened to save the tribal boy from the clutches of a tiger, ultimately vanquishing the beast.

Overwhelmed by grief at the loss of his comrades, the prince beseeched the divine intervention of Lord Shiva. Moved by the prince's earnest prayers, Shiva appeared before him and granted his plea, miraculously resurrecting the fallen men. In gratitude for this divine intervention, the prince vowed to erect a temple in honor of Lord Shiva at the site where his prayers were answered.

Eka listens to the tale with a knowing smile playing on his lips, recognising the embellishments woven into the narrative. He suppresses a chuckle as he reminisces about a humorous incident from his own childhood.

"Why do you wear such a mischievous grin, guruji?" inquires one of his disciples, curious about Eka's reaction.

With a twinkle in his eye, Eka responds, "Oh, that tale of the prince and the tribal boy... it simply reminded me of a comical childhood anecdote."

Taking leave of the temple after receiving the divine blessings, Eka's gaze falls upon a young child engrossed in prayer before the idol. Struck by a sense of familiarity, he attempts to recall where he may have encountered the child before, but the memory eludes him.

Despite the reluctance of his disciples, Eka insists they leave him alone, their disapproval evident in their expressions. Unfazed by their concerns about the jungle's wild inhabitants, Eka possesses an intimate knowledge of the forest, having once been its apex predator.

With ease, he navigates the dense foliage, memories flooding back as he ventures deeper into the wilderness. Eventually, he arrives at his abandoned home, a decrepit wooden structure lost amidst the expanse of trees. Nearby lies a poignant reminder of the past—a necklace of fingers, now reduced to mere bones.

Approaching the burnt door adorned with a fading painting of Lord Shiva, Eka offers a solemn prayer, seeking forgiveness for the turmoil he once unleashed upon the world.

"Forgive me, my lord, for the destruction I have wrought," he murmurs, his words a whispered plea amidst the quiet of the forest.

Gathering his father's ashes, Eka pays his respects at the makeshift memorial, the weight of his grief palpable in the air. Before departing, he places markers around the grave, ensuring that his father's resting place remains undisturbed, even as the landscape may shift and change in the future.

□

Chapter 14

1100 A.D. – GOD of War

The Present

"I will continue the story tomorrow. It's time for you to sleep," says the old man.

"Please continue," the kid requests.

"I'm sorry, Omkar. It's sleep time. I even got you chocolate. Listen to me for once," the grandfather gently insists.

"What if I sleep and don't wake up? I want this story to be the last one I hear, Grandpa," pleads the boy.

"Please don't say such things. I love you. I will continue the story. Don't lose hope, Omkar," says the grandfather, his voice filled with love and concern.

"I'm sorry," says Omkar.

In the serene ambiance of Kashi, Eka stands on the sacred banks of the Ganges, surrounded by his devoted disciples. The river flows gently, its waters whispering ancient secrets as they cascade over smooth stones.

With a heavy heart and trembling hands, Eka holds the container of his father's ashes, feeling the weight of centuries-old regrets and unspoken apologies. He speaks softly, his words carried away by the gentle breeze.

"Sorry for taking my time, Dad. I hope you forgive me for the things I have done," he murmurs, his voice laden with emotion. "As promised, I am mixing your ashes in the Ganges... even though I am many years late. Give me a sign, suggesting you are happy with my change."

Closing his eyes, Eka offers a heartfelt prayer to his departed father, seeking solace and redemption in the sacred waters of the holy river. With a steady hand, he begins to scatter the ashes into the flowing currents, watching as they merge with the shimmering surface of the Ganges.

As he performs the solemn ritual, Eka's gaze drifts upwards towards the expansive sky, searching for a sign of approval from the heavens above. In that moment, a sense of peace washes over him, as if his father's spirit is watching over him with a comforting presence.

Amidst the poignant scene, Eka's attention is drawn to the figure of a saffron-clad monk holding a small metallic container adorned with a striking red gemstone near the river. Recognition sparks in his eyes as he realises it is the same monk who once saved his life.

With a sense of gratitude and reverence, Eka smiles and lifts his hands in silent thanks to the gods for guiding him on this transformative journey. As he turns to acknowledge the saffron-clad monk, his heart filled with curiosity and a yearning for answers, he calls out to him with a voice tinged with urgency and determination.

"Hey, monk!" Eka's voice echoes across the tranquil surroundings, but the monk seems unaffected, his gaze fixed ahead as he continues on his path. Undeterred, Eka quickens his pace, determined to unravel the mystery that surrounds the enigmatic figure.

Through winding streets and bustling thoroughfares, Eka follows the monk's trail, his footsteps echoing against the ancient walls of the city. The streets are alive with the vibrant tapestry of life, each corner adorned with the colours and sounds of Kashi's rich heritage.

Finally, they arrive at the majestic Kashi Vishwanath Temple, its towering spires reaching towards the heavens in silent reverence. The temple stands as a timeless symbol of devotion and spirituality, its sacred precincts thronged with pilgrims and seekers from all walks of life.

As Eka's disciples trail behind him, their faces reflecting a mixture of awe and confusion, they struggle to keep pace with their master amidst the bustling crowd. In the midst of the bustling throng, Eka's figure becomes lost to their sight, swallowed by the sea of devotees who flock to the temple in search of divine blessings and solace.

Upon arriving at the Kashi Viswanath temple, the grandeur of its interiors captivates Eka. Intricately carved pillars adorned with ancient motifs line the spacious halls, leading to the sanctum where the divine Shivling resides, radiating a serene aura.

Inside, amidst the hushed reverence of worshippers, Eka searches for the monk but finds no trace. As he explores further, his gaze falls upon a young boy deep in prayer before the Shivling—a sight that evokes a sense of déjà vu. The boy's profound spiritual presence fills the sanctum with an ethereal energy, reminiscent of ages past.

Turning his attention elsewhere, Eka spots the monk preparing to rest in the tranquil garden nearby. Determined, he strides towards the monk, his heart heavy with anticipation.

Eka respectfully approaches the monk, his voice echoing through the hallowed silence of the temple. The monk, clad in humble robes, bears the marks of life's trials. Despite Eka's greeting, the monk remains absorbed in his meditation, seemingly indifferent to his presence.

Undeterred, Eka steps back, allowing the monk the space he seeks for his spiritual practice. With patience born of reverence, Eka observes in silence as the monk begins to chant sacred Shiva mantras, each syllable resonating with divine power.

As the final echoes of the mantras fade, the monk opens his eyes, meeting Eka's gaze with a silent acknowledgment. Gathering his belongings, the monk prepares to depart, his purposeful strides marking the beginning of a new journey.

"Wait, noble monk," Eka entreats, his voice tinged with earnestness. "I seek your wisdom. Will you not converse with me?"

The monk ignores him and strides forward, Eka follows behind, the thick jungle canopy surrounding them. The only sounds accompanying them are the rustling leaves and the chirping of birds, as Eka's disciples are nowhere to be found.

Eventually, the monk finds shelter beneath a towering peepal tree, resting his weary body. Eka settles nearby, but the monk pays him no attention, lost in slumber.

At dawn, Eka wakes to find the monk already deep in prayer by the tranquil waters. After completing his devotions, the monk retrieves some berries from his bag, gathered during his travels.

Eka's stomach grumbles with hunger, and sensing this, the monk offers him a piece of fruit. Grateful for the gesture, Eka accepts and eagerly eats, feeling refreshed by the nourishment.

Their journey continues, leading them to another sacred site, where Eka's father once sought solace in prayer. While the monk resumes his devotions, Eka ventures into the lush jungle, gathering fruits and berries to share with his silent companion.

Eka returns with a handful of fruits and finds the monk deeply immersed in meditation before the sacred lingam. He patiently waits for the monk to conclude his meditative state. The next day, as the monk opens his eyes, he is surprised to see Eka applying herbal paste to his wounds. Reacting abruptly, he kicks Eka.

"What are you doing?" the monk exclaims.

"I apologise, master. I am applying this medicine to aid in healing your wounds," Eka responds.

"They won't work on my wounds," the monk declares.

"I have learned from some of the finest medical practitioners in ancient India. Your wounds can be healed," Eka reassures.

"These are not ordinary wounds. They are eternal curses," the monk solemnly states.

Intrigued, Eka inquires further, "What do you mean by eternal curses, revered monk?"

Without offering a direct response, the monk rises and begins to walk away, with Eka following closely behind.

"Where are we headed, monk?" inquires Eka.

"I walk alone. I wish for you to cease following me," responds the monk.

"How can I, monk? I have searched for you for millennia," Eka replies.

The monk is taken aback. "Have you been drinking toddy this morning?" he growls.

Undeterred, Eka continues to follow the monk as he walks.

"I gave up such vices when Buddha granted me spiritual awakening," Eka explains.

"If you are a Buddhist, why do you pray to Shiva?" questions the monk.

"Thanks to Shankaracharya, I have returned to Hinduism," Eka replies.

"Your stories may be intriguing, but I have no association with you. I forge my own path," asserts the monk.

"Perhaps you may not be connected to me, but my existence is intertwined with yours," Eka asserts confidently.

The monk gazes at Eka, perplexed by his words.

"Now if your ranting is completed, I have to pray to Lord Shiva," growls the monk.

"Why do you pray to the Lord when you yourself are a god?" questions Eka.

Feeling threatened, the monk responds, "What are you talking about?"

"I am speaking the truth. You saved my life 2,500 years ago when you blessed me with a long life, and amrit from your vessel accidentally fell into my mouth," Eka replies.

"You are good at telling stories. I'll give you that. But even if you're correct, what is the proof that you aren't lying?" asks the monk.

"I remember the vessel. A lingam-shaped vessel embedded with red gemstones. I know it's the same vessel, but you have lost the gemstones. 2,500 years ago, you carried the same vessel," Eka explains, pointing at the rusty vessel.

"I got this vessel in a market in Kashi two years ago. I am just a wandering beggar, so kindly leave me alone," the monk responds.

"Your height. I haven't seen any monks as tall as you," Eka says. "Then you haven't traveled the world," replies the monk.

"I know you are an immortal. I can prove it if you remove your head scarf," roars Eka.

Worried, the monk ignores him and starts walking away.

"Don't you dare run away from the conversation. I know who you are," Eka insists.

The monk looks back at him. "Who am I?" he asks.

Amidst the sacred ambiance of the temple, the atmosphere crackled with tension as Eka confronted the mysterious monk. With fervour in his voice, Eka unleashed a torrent of revelations, weaving a tale of ancient legend and divine retribution.

"You are no ordinary wanderer, monk. You are one of the Astha Chiranjeevi, the Eight Immortals! Born with a jewel on your forehead, blessed by Mahadeva and the penance of Drona," Eka declared, his words echoing through the forest.

"Endowed with the divine jewel, you wielded dominion over all creatures beneath humanity's realm. This sacred gem shielded you from the pangs of hunger, thirst, and weariness. Born to Guru Drona and Kripi, sister of Kripacharya, you reigned over the northern expanse of Panchala with wisdom and might," Eka continued, his voice resonating with reverence.

"Your prowess rivaled that of Arjuna, particularly in the art of archery. In a legendary battle, you clashed with Arjuna to a standstill, achieving the remarkable feat of severing the string of his mighty Gandiva bow. During the tumultuous events of the 14th night of the Mahabharata, when Ghatotkacha wrought havoc upon the Kaurava forces and none could halt his rampage, it was you who emerged triumphant. In a fateful confrontation, you vanquished Ghatotkacha and struck down his son Anjanparvan before his very eyes. The unjust demise of Drona and Duryodhana ignited a fierce transformation within you, fueling a thirst for vengeance. Under the veil of darkness, you launched a savage assault on the Pandava encampment, swiftly eliminating Drishtadyumna, Shikhandi, the Upapandavas, and countless other valiant warriors of the Pandava army. It was during this tumultuous time that the divine presence of Mahadeva infused your being, bestowing upon you the divine sword as the era of the Panchalas on Earth drew to a close. In this incarnation, you embodied the formidable Rudra avatar of Shiva, wielding unparalleled power and ferocity in your quest for retribution," praised Eka, his admiration evident in every word.

"You possess mastery over weaponry beyond compare. In a dire moment of peril, you unleashed the formidable Brahmashira, channeling its destructive force through a humble blade of grass to shield yourself from harm. However, your action prompted Arjuna to deploy his own Brahmashira in defense, resulting in a clash of divine forces that threatened cataclysmic devastation. In a decisive intervention, the sage Vyasa halted the catastrophic trajectory of both celestial weapons. While Arjuna successfully withdrew his Brahmashira, you, regrettably, failed to retract yours. Tragically, in a moment of misguided fury, you directed the lethal force towards Uttara, the wife of Abhimanyu, committing a grievous transgression that reverberated throughout the ages," Eka continued, his voice tinged with sorrow.

"Bhagwan Sri Krishna considered this act as the gravest violation of righteousness within the Mahabharata saga, leading to the forfeiture of the divine gem from your forehead. In righteous indignation, he condemned you to wander the earth for three millennia, your being afflicted with perpetual oozing of blood and pus. I am aware of your identity, noble monk," Eka affirmed, his tone solemn and resolute.

"A solitary monk, journeying from one sacred Shiva temple to another, devoutly devoted to the deity, is a sight to behold. He bears a sword within his backpack, a silent testament to his past. Boils mar his once unblemished skin, and a distinctive wound, shaped like a diamond, marks his forehead. Since the era of the Mahabharata, he has traversed the lands of Bharata, his cursed fate intertwined with the annals of history. Cursed by the divine Lord Krishna himself for the heinous act of slaying the Pandavas' scion, he bears the burden of an eternal wanderer. Yet, amidst his afflictions, he remains a master of arms, his prowess unmatched in the annals of time. Indeed, my lord, you are none other than the illustrious Ashwatthama," Eka proclaimed, his voice echoing with reverence and awe.

"I am indebted to you for saving my life and bestowing upon me the gift of immortality," pleaded Eka with profound gratitude in his voice. "Please allow me to journey alongside you, to explore the world and glean wisdom from your experiences."

With tears of reverence welling in his eyes, Eka humbly prostrated himself before Ashwatthama, his forehead touching the ground in a gesture of deep respect.

Moved by Eka's heartfelt plea, Ashwatthama gently raised him up, acknowledging the sincerity of his request. Together, they stood, one mortal and one immortal, united by a shared journey filled with the promise of discovery and enlightenment.

"I was never supposed to grant you immortality, but what is done is done," Ashwatthama's voice resonated with a heavy burden of remorse. "I am cursed to walk alone, a punishment for my sins. Hence, I cannot take you along with me. However, we shall meet on this same day in 100 years' time," he declared with a sense of inevitability.

Eka, understanding the weight of Ashwatthama's words, folded his hands in acceptance.

"Yes, my lord, we shall meet. But where?" Eka inquired, his gaze filled with curiosity.

Ashwatthama surveyed the surroundings before responding, "The temple started by your father seems like a perfect place to meet. You have a personal connection to it, and the place itself emanates positive energy."

With reverence, Eka fell at Ashwatthama's feet once again, seeking his blessings. Ashwatthama graciously blessed him before preparing to depart.

"See you in 100 years from now, Eka," Ashwatthama bid farewell.

"See you in the year 1226, my lord," Eka replied, his voice filled with anticipation for the destined reunion.

□

Chapter 15

Bharat 1226 A.D. – The Chola Mason

The Present

The old man's phone suddenly rings, and he quickly steps away to take the call, ensuring privacy. Meanwhile, the young boy, Omkar, eagerly awaits the continuation of the story.

"Grandfather, why did you stop telling the story? It was getting super exciting," Omkar asks with enthusiasm.

Mohan, the old man, responds softly, "Your father is coming."

Upon hearing this, Omkar's face lights up with joy. "Did he find me a cure? He promised me he would find a cure," the boy exclaims, his excitement palpable.

"I'm sure he did," Mohan reassures him, offering words of comfort.

Just then, Eka enters the room, dressed impeccably in a stylish suit and sporting sunglasses. Though his appearance may have changed from ancient India, his aura exudes a level of sophistication and confidence beyond compare. The nurse, requests Eka for a selfie, but he politely declines, citing the hospital setting.

Upon seeing Eka, both Mohan and Omkar burst into excited cheers, thrilled by his arrival.

Mohan's voice trembles with emotion as he expresses his longing for his son. "Dad, I have missed you," he tells Eka, his eyes moist with tears. Eka, moved by his Mohan's words, embraces him warmly, offering comfort and solace in their reunion.

"Did you get the amrut?" Mohan inquires, his hope evident in his voice. Eka's expression shifts, a veil of sadness descending upon his face as he remains silent, unable to fulfill Mohan's expectations.

Sensing disappointment, Eka returns the embrace, offering silent reassurance and understanding before turning his attention to Omkar, the young boy filled with uncertainty and fear.

"Dad, will I live? Is God going to save me?" Omkar's voice quivers with vulnerability as he holds out a rudraksha bead in his hand, seeking answers and solace from his father figure.

Gently taking Omkar's hand, Eka meets his gaze with a mixture of compassion and wisdom. "There are only two ways to live your life. One is as though nothing is a miracle. The other is as though everything is a miracle," he shares, his words carrying a profound sense of conviction and hope.

"Don't worry, son," Eka continues, his voice filled with reassurance. "I have witnessed many miracles in my life, and it's not God who is going to save you. It is you, Dad, who will save you."

Moved by Eka's words of encouragement, Omkar's face lights up with a radiant smile, his fears momentarily eased by the belief in his father's strength and resilience. With a heartfelt embrace, father and son share a moment of profound connection and love, united in their journey to overcome adversity together.

Eka sits regally at the entrance of the grand temple, his demeanour exuding a newfound sense of refinement and authority. Dressed in attire befitting his royal stature, he appears markedly transformed, with meticulously groomed hair and a neatly trimmed beard that speaks of his dignified presence. A guard stands nearby, dutifully shielding him from the sun with an umbrella, a symbol of his elevated status.

The path leading to the temple is lined with rows of majestic trees, their branches swaying gently in the breeze, while a steady stream of devotees forms a queue, patiently awaiting their turn to enter the sacred space. Amidst this bustling scene, a priest approaches Eka with deference, urging him to wait indoors until his expected guest arrives.

"Sir, please wait inside. We will inform you when your guest arrives," the priest advises respectfully.

But Eka, resolute in his determination, declines the offer, his eyes fixed on the horizon in anticipation. "No, I have waited a long time for this man. I must receive him myself," he insists firmly, his voice carrying a note of quiet conviction.

The priest, deferential to Eka's wishes, inquires if there is anything else he requires. "Do you need anything else, sir?" he asks, eager to attend to Eka's needs.

Eka, however, reassures the priest, urging him to proceed with the temple rituals without concern for his presence. "Carry on with the pujas. Don't worry about me. Please, accompany this gentleman," he instructs, gesturing toward the servant who had been holding the umbrella.

As the servant departs, Eka's gaze suddenly alights upon a figure approaching, a frail yet unmistakable presence. With a surge of recognition, he realises that his long-awaited guest has finally arrived–none other than Ashwatthama himself, unchanged by the passage of a century.

Without hesitation, Eka rushes forward to greet him, his heart brimming with reverence and gratitude. Falling to his knees before Ashwatthama, he offers humble obeisance, his actions a poignant display of respect and reverence. Moved by Eka's heartfelt gesture, Ashwatthama gently lifts him up, their reunion marked by a profound exchange of mutual respect and admiration. In a symbolic gesture of honour, Eka places the umbrella atop Ashwatthama's head, a gesture of reverence befitting the noble presence before him.

"Well, this place looks beautiful," remarks Ashwatthama, his eyes scanning the grandeur of the temple.

"I'm glad you liked it. I had to rebuild everything and remodel the entire temple structure," responds Eka with a hint of pride in his voice.

"So, how have the last 100 years been for you, and what exactly do you do now?" inquires Ashwatthama.

"I build temples for kings," replies Eka succinctly.

"I assumed you were a hunter," remarks Ashwatthama, curiosity gleaming in his eyes.

"Hunting was indeed a thrilling pursuit, but I knew I would always remain a shudra. That realisation led me southward, where I discovered the magnificence of the Chola kings, renowned for their rule and architecture. Witnessing their temples and maritime prowess left me awe-struck. It was then I made a decision: to either construct temples or ships. Given my familial connection to temple construction, courtesy of my father's small temple, I chose the former path."

"I learnt the art of temple design and construction from the skilled Chola masons, who were impressed by my dedication and skills. Although they urged me to stay, my heart yearned to return home to reunite with you. Initially, I started by rebuilding small temples scattered across the land. Then, I embarked on the monumental task of refurbishing this very Shiva temple. My efforts caught the eye of the king, who rewarded me with a substantial tract of land—500 acres, to be precise. Some of it I acquired independently, while others were graciously bestowed by the king himself."

"Now, I dedicate myself to building temples for our king, but this temple holds a special place in my heart—it's my own personal project," concludes Eka, his voice brimming with pride and fulfillment.

"Come with me, I will show you something interesting," Eka beckons, leading Ashwatthama towards a particular spot near the temple's base.

Pointing to an inscription etched into the stone, Eka explains, "It reads, 'Dedicated to Lord Shiva, built by Ekagraha Aahuk.'"

Ashwatthama's curiosity is piqued. "So, you have retained a part of your name and added your father's name as well," he observes.

With a proud smile, Eka nods. "Indeed. I plan to honour my father's memory by constructing his tomb on this land and ensuring its renown," he declares.

As Ashwatthama gazes up at the sky, a hint of anticipation in the air, he suggests, "Let us go inside. Rain is imminent."

Eka glances skyward, puzzled by Ashwatthama's statement. "What rain? It's blistering hot," he questions.

"I can smell the rain," Ashwatthama insists confidently, leading the way into the temple. They encounter some resistance from the priests, who halt the commoners from entering.

"Why are you stopping the devotees?" Ashwatthama queries.

"For your prayers," Eka responds, gesturing for the guards to allow the devotees to proceed.

Ashwatthama interjects, "Their prayers are the same as mine."

With Eka's signal, the guards step aside, allowing the devotees to enter alongside them. Inside, Ashwatthama joins the worshippers in prayer. Meanwhile, Eka notices a familiar sight: the small boy he has seen in the queue multiple times over the centuries.

Suddenly, rain begins to fall, surprising Eka. With a smile, he marvels at the sight, feeling a sense of wonder at the unexpected weather.

Exiting the temple, Ashwatthama is greeted by a downpour. Undeterred, Eka follows, sheltering him with an umbrella as they navigate through the rain-drenched surroundings.

"Where are you going? Please stay here until the rain stops," Eka pleads, concern evident in his voice.

"It won't stop for three days," Ashwatthama replies, his tone resigned to the inevitability of the downpour.

"Let me come with you... I beg you," Eka implores, desperate to accompany his enigmatic companion.

Ashwatthama begins to walk away, rain pouring down relentlessly.

"At least tell me, how did you know it was going to rain?" Eka shouts over the din of the pelting rain, his words lost amidst the downpour.

“When you live for eternity, you start using all your sensory organs to the fullest... You feel the smells of nature,” Ashwatthama shouts back, his voice barely audible amidst the deluge.

“Can I come with you?” Eka’s request hangs in the air, hopeful yet uncertain.

Ignoring Eka’s plea, Ashwatthama simply states, “See you in 1319, same place, same time,” before disappearing into the rain-soaked horizon.

□

Chapter 16

Bharat 1326 A.D. – The King

The Present

Eka stands beside Omkar and the grandfather, the weight of their conversation heavy in the air.

"Why didn't Eka become a Brahmin?" the curious kid asks, his innocence shining through.

"You want non-veg every day, but you want Eka to eat only veg for 100 years," Eka playfully replies, a hint of amusement in his voice.

The kid chuckles at Eka's response, his young mind grasping the humor in the situation.

"Here, it's time for your food and medicine," Mohan interjects, trying to distract the kid from his worries.

But the kid remains distraught, his mind grappling with unanswered questions.

"Dad, I have a doubt," the kid speaks up, seeking clarity amidst his confusion.

"Have your medicines, and I will clarify all your doubts," Eka assures, his voice gentle yet firm.

With a grimace, the kid reluctantly swallows his medicine, preparing himself for the forthcoming explanation.

"I don't even remember what happened in last week's exams... How come Eka remembers his dad's face and name after 2,500 years?" the kid's doubt lingers in the air, his brow furrowed in contemplation.

"Selective memory... Will you forget my face if you

don't see me for a year?" Eka counters, offering a simple yet profound explanation.

The kid's expression softens as understanding dawns upon him, nodding in agreement with Eka's reasoning.

"Something similar to that. Now, let's continue with the story," Eka gently redirects the conversation, eager to delve back into the captivating tale.

Ashwatthama strides towards the temple, marvelling at its grandeur compared to what he saw a century ago. However, his progress is halted by the guards stationed at a makeshift checkpoint.

"You are not allowed inside, beggar!" one of the guards barks, his tone laced with disdain.

Another guard quickly intervenes, offering apologies to Ashwatthama and granting him passage.

"Apologies, sir. Kindly pass through," the second guard urges respectfully.

With a nod of acknowledgment, Ashwatthama proceeds forward, though the interaction leaves him puzzled.

"Why did you let that beggar pass?" the first guard questions his companion.

"Didn't they inform us to let tall men pass today?" comes the nonchalant reply.

"What if spies pass through?" the first guard persists, expressing concern.

"Not our problem," the other guard retorts dismissively, the pair sharing a laugh as Ashwatthama continues on his way, noting the heightened security measures surrounding the temple.

As he approaches the majestic Nandi statue adorning the temple entrance, Ashwatthama is greeted by a familiar voice. Turning around, he sees his old friend, Eka.

"It's fantastic, isn't it?" Eka inquires, his demeanour exuding confidence and elegance.

Ashwatthama nods in agreement, his attention drawn to Eka's refined appearance. Dressed lavishly and accompanied by a retinue of guards, Eka descends gracefully from a chariot. He asks his subordinates to leave.

"You look fancy," Ashwatthama remarks, acknowledging Eka's distinguished attire and regal demeanour.

"I am the king of this land. The king didn't have any sons, so he married one of his daughters to me," Eka explains with a sense of pride, presenting a painting depicting his opulent wedding. Ashwatthama smiles warmly at the depiction, intrigued by the story behind it.

"Why do you smile?" Eka inquires, curious about his friend's reaction to the painting.

"This man doesn't look anything like you. You are not so muscular or tall," Ashwatthama observes, noting the disparity between the depicted prince and Eka's own appearance.

"History is always marred by lies. When I inquired about the history of this temple, a priest showed me a painting. In it, a valiant prince is depicted hunting a ferocious tiger and rescuing a tribal boy from imminent danger. I was that tribal boy, but what happened was completely different," Eka reveals, shedding light on the discrepancies in historical narratives. "These painters always exaggerate."

Ashwatthama nods in understanding, recognising the tendency to embellish tales in historical records.

"So, what did you do that impressed the king and led him to make you his son-in-law?" Ashwatthama inquires, intrigued by Eka's rise to royalty.

"Again, thanks to you," Eka responds, causing Ashwatthama to express surprise.

"Do you know that most of northern India is now in control of the invaders?" Eka asks, shifting the conversation to a more somber topic.

Ashwatthama nods, acknowledging the ongoing conflicts with invaders.

"Those bastards dare to come here to our lands. The invaders camped on the dried riverbed, 100 kilometers from here, on the outskirts of the holy city of Kashi. It didn't rain for 20 years, and the river was almost dry, leading to severe drought," Eka recounts the dire situation, his tone reflecting the gravity of the circumstances.

"My king was charging to battle when he heard that the invaders destroyed the Vishveshwara Temple and built a mosque over it. We were angry, as they destroyed a famous temple and afterwards razed the city of Kashi.

We were 5,000 men against their 10,000. They had cavalry and war elephants. Yet, we wanted to fight and kill them," Eka explains passionately. "But when I reached the battlefield, I sensed a change."I requested my king to wait for two days. Everyone laughed at me, calling me a coward. I begged them all to give me two days," Eka continues, recounting his bold decision.

"And why is that?" Ashwatthama inquires, curious about Eka's unusual request.

"I could smell the rain," Eka reveals, emphasising his heightened senses and intuition.

"The king thought I was a traitor, but I pleaded with him, and we waited. On the third day, the invaders were washed away by the Ganga, as if the river was cleansing away the filth. Maybe their sins of destroying the temple got to them We didn't even have to fight," Eka explains with a chuckle. "The king thought I had some kind of blessings given by the gods, and he made me his son-in-law."

"Your life seems happy and prosperous," Ashwatthama observes, intrigued by Eka's journey from humble beginnings to royal status, his admiration evident in his tone.

"I am happy on the outside, but I am very sad," confesses Eka, his demeanour reflecting a hidden sorrow.

"Why is that?" asks Ashwatthama, concerned by his friend's admission.

"I am unable to father children. I have tried all the yagnas and pujas, but nothing has happened," Eka reveals, his voice tinged with disappointment.

Ashwatthama's expression turns grave as he absorbs the news.

"You will never have children, Eka," he states bluntly.

Surprised and disheartened, Eka seeks clarification. "Why do you say that?" he asks, his tone tinged with disbelief.

"Brahma hasn't written anything in your fate. You were supposed to die, but thanks to luck, you have survived. Thus, you won't have kids in this lifetime, and by this lifetime, I mean for eternity," Ashwatthama explains solemnly, delivering a harsh truth.

Eka's spirits sink further upon hearing Ashwatthama's words. He grapples with the weight of this revelation, feeling a sense of loss for something he may never have.

"Well, if Brahma hasn't written my fate, it looks like I will have to write my own fate, which will make even Brahma jealous," Eka declares defiantly, his determination shining through his sorrow.

But Ashwatthama warns him sternly, "Have humility, Ekagraha Aahuk. Don't try to mess with the gods."

Undeterred, Eka asserts his newfound identity. "I am Ekanayaka Raja Raja now, taken from the names of Shiva and the greatest Hindu king of India. Can't have a Vaishya name. I am a Kshatriya now," he declares with conviction.

Curious, Ashwatthama inquires, "Didn't anyone have a doubt seeing you don't really age?"

Eka responds with a hint of mischief in his voice, "I passed off as my own son twice. Though some people in my kingdom think I am a bastard child who stole the throne. But I can always get rid of them." His words carry a subtle warning, hinting at the power he wields as a ruler.

Amidst the sacred confines of the temple, Ashwatthama raises a pertinent question, his gaze drifting to the vigilant soldiers stationed nearby.

"Why do you have so much security?" he asks, noting the formidable garrison surrounding the temple.

"We have to be vigilant for catching spies from neighboring kingdoms. Some of them have joined hands with outsiders. Can't trust anyone these days," Eka responds, his expression tinged with concern for the safety of the sacred space.

"But they can't kill you," Ashwatthama points out, acknowledging Eka's formidable reputation.

Eka, however, gestures toward the opulent surroundings with a somber expression. "But they can take away all this," he states, his words carrying the weight of the responsibilities he bears.

Ashwatthama offers a knowing smile, recognising the complexities of Eka's predicament. "Looks like you are addicted to wealth and the good life," he remarks, his tone gentle yet probing.

Eka, however, counters with a thoughtful question. "Without this wealth, how can I be of service to God or the people?" he queries, revealing his deep-rooted sense of duty and responsibility.

"Hard times create strong men. Strong men create good times. Good times create weak men. And, weak men create hard times. That's the circle of life," Ashwatthama reflects, imparting timeless wisdom. "Don't let good times make you weak."

"I will keep that in mind, my lord," Eka responds respectfully, absorbing Ashwatthama's sage advice.

As Ashwatthama begins his prayers, Eka waits patiently, a sense of reverence enveloping the tranquil ambiance of the temple. Once the prayers are complete, Ashwatthama descends the temple stairs, his footsteps echoing a sense of timeless wisdom and quiet strength.

"Are you already leaving?" Eka's voice carries a note of reluctance as he watches Ashwatthama prepare to depart.

Ashwatthama nods solemnly in response.

"Please come to my palace and relax for a few days. You can experience my hospitality," Eka urges, his plea infused with genuine warmth.

"You seem to forget that I was once the king of Panchala," Ashwatthama replies with a hint of nostalgia in his voice.

"I didn't mean it in that way. We only meet once in a hundred years. I want you to stay for a couple more days," Eka insists, his desire for Ashwatthama's company palpable.

As Ashwatthama begins to walk away, Eka makes one last attempt. "At least take a few of my men with you. They will help you," he suggests earnestly.

Ashwatthama pauses, glancing back at Eka. "See you in 1419 at the same place, O king," he says with a faint smile, acknowledging Eka's current royalty.

"Please wait. At least tell me the place where I can find amrut?" Eka's plea halts Ashwatthama in his tracks, his question catching him off guard.

He shows Ashwatthama a pendant adorned with a photo of a lady. "She is the only one I have loved. She is my adopted daughter... everyone I know dies, while I continue to live. I want to make her immortal like me," Eka explains, his anguish evident.

"Do you feel guilty when you see everybody you love die in front of you?" Ashwatthama inquires gently, his voice filled with empathy.

"I do, but I can't do anything... You don't know the pain when people close to us keep dying... Help me, please. I don't even know if I am cursed or blessed," Eka pleads, his vulnerability laid bare.

Ashwatthama's smile is bittersweet as he listens to Eka's heartfelt plea. "You said you would build a tomb for your father," he recalls, changing the subject.

"I searched for a hundred years for his tombstone. I couldn't find the place where he was killed... The landscape is changing rapidly," Eka admits with a hint of sorrow.

"How do you expect me to know the original location of where *amrut* was churned? That happened during the Mahabharata millennia ago," Ashwatthama replies, his words carrying a sense of resignation.

Eka nods in understanding, his expression reflecting a mixture of acceptance and determination.

"It makes sense... But if I search long enough, can I find it?" Eka's question is laced with a hint of determination.

"Do you think you are the only person who tried to find the location of the *amrut*? Many kings tried finding it before you, and many will try after you... One lifetime isn't sufficient to find nature's blessings," Ashwatthama remarks, his tone carrying the weight of experience.

"Well, I have all the time in the world," Eka retorts with a confident smirk.

Ashwatthama smiles knowingly, acknowledging Eka's immortality.

"Finding this *amrut* may be my purpose, my mission in life," Eka declares with a sense of resolve.

"See you, Eka... I hope you fulfil your mission," Ashwatthama bids farewell, his words carrying a sense of encouragement.

□

Chapter 17

Bharat 1423 A.D. – Amrut

The Present

Eka stands near the bed with Omkar and Mohan, listening to their curious musings.

"Why couldn't Eka find his father's grave? I'm only 10 years old, and I know the way to KFC or Playzone. Are ancient people dumb?" Omkar questions with youthful innocence.

Eka can't help but smile at the boy's candid inquiry. "But there was no KFC or Playzone during that time," he explains gently.

Interrupting their conversation, Mohan interjects with a thoughtful response. "Ancient people aren't dumb. They knew much more than us... These Lord Shiva temples were constructed 4,000 years ago by ancient architects in an era without satellite technology or GPS. Yet, these temples were accurately established at 79° longitudes."

Mohan opens his phone and shows them a webpage, illustrating his point. "Look at this. The distance between Kedarnath and Rameswaram is 2,383 kilometers."

He continues, pointing to various temple locations. "Kedarnath at 79.0669°, Kalahashti at 79.7037°, Ekambaranatha in Kanchi at 79.7036°, Thiruvanamalai at 79.0747°, Thiruvanaikaval at 78.7108°, Chidambaram Nataraja at 79.6954°, Rameshwaram at 79.3129°, and Kaleshwaram in North India at 79.9067°."

"Our ancestors were geniuses. We don't acknowledge

their intelligence as much as they deserve," Mohan concludes with admiration for ancient ingenuity.

Eka, sensing the seriousness of the conversation, decides to lighten the mood. "Seems like Eka is a fool living among the ancient people... He isn't as smart as you and your grandfather," he jokes, eliciting laughter from Omkar.

The room fills with light-hearted amusement, blending wisdom and humour in their shared moments.

Amidst the tranquil ambiance of the temple garden, Eka and Ashwatthama engage in conversation, surrounded by the soothing sounds of chirping birds and the gentle flow of water from a nearby pond. Children frolic in the water, adding to the serene atmosphere. Eka, appearing even more fashionable, exudes an air of refinement.

Ashwatthama admires the new addition to the temple. "The water body is a nice addition."

"It just started accumulating here mysteriously... No one knows how or why. Then I had a bund built around it. Locals believe Lord Shiva created a water-producing spot here, hence the name Janvapi," explains Eka, sharing the local legend.

"Do you believe what people say?" Ashwatthama inquires.

"Who am I to question their faith? With reforestation efforts around the temple, water began to accumulate here. Maybe it truly is Shiva's blessing upon the place," muses Eka, embracing the mystical aura.

Ashwatthama smiles, acknowledging the power of belief.

"This may soon become one of the biggest Shiva temples in India," predicts Eka, envisioning the temple's grandeur.

"It seems like you're reserving your place in Shivaloka," remarks Ashwatthama, recognising Eka's devotion.

"Whatever Mahadev commands," Eka responds, gazing skyward with reverence.

Ashwatthama notices Eka's ability to seamlessly blend into different roles. "Seems like you've also become efficient in passing off as your own son," he remarks.

Eka chuckles. "What's your name now?" Ashwatthama asks.

"I am Ekanayaka Raja Raja the third," Eka proudly declares, sharing his regal title.

Their laughter fills the air, bridging the gap between ancient traditions and modern humour.

As they enter the temple, they pray together to Shiva. The priest offers temple food on a plate, and Ashwatthama partakes while Eka declines.

"Why didn't you take the prasadam?" Ashwatthama asks.

"After eating the same prasad for 100 years, one tends to get bored. I will go home and eat," Eka replies with a lighthearted smile, reflecting his familiarity with the temple rituals.

They observe a young boy deeply immersed in prayer, his familiar presence catching Eka's attention.

"The boy looks familiar. Looks like I've seen him somewhere," remarks Eka, his curiosity piqued.

Ashwatthama inquires, "Ask him who he is."

"He must be some priest's son," Eka suggests, noting the boy's intense focus on his prayers.

Changing the subject, Ashwatthama asks about matters of war and kingdom affairs.

"What about conflicts or the affairs of your kingdom?" inquires Ashwatthama.

"In these good times, Ashwatthama, we revel in peace, prosperity, learning, and religion. Let's hope nothing disrupts this harmony," Eka responds optimistically.

"In my travels, I've witnessed Bharat being threatened by invaders," Ashwatthama warns, expressing concerns about external threats.

"They won't dare to set foot in my kingdom. They fear me," Eka asserts confidently, displaying his resolve to protect his realm.

Ashwatthama shifts the conversation to Eka's quest for the *amrut*.

"What about your pursuit of the *amrut*?" inquires Ashwatthama.

"I've delved into every book and scripture, sent my best men to locate the Mandara Mountain, but to no avail. They've either vanished or been captured by the enemy," Eka admits with a hint of frustration.

"Did you come close to finding the location at least?" Ashwatthama inquires sympathetically.

"My men believe the Mandara Mountain lies in the Bondhi district of Magadha. However, upon reaching there, we found no trace of the Ksheera Sagara, let alone a nearby river," Eka laments, revealing the setbacks in his quest.

"Perhaps, like the Saraswati River, even the Ksheera Sagara has disappeared," he muses, drawing parallels with ancient phenomena.

Eka gestures towards the Janvapi lake, emphasising its mystical allure. "That's why this water body holds even more significance."

"For now, I've set aside my quest for *amrut*. My focus is on building temples and safeguarding my people from invaders," Eka declares, showcasing his commitment to his kingdom's welfare.

Ashwatthama's smile carries a mix of relief and understanding. "I am relieved to hear that you have chosen to step away from this daunting quest," he says gently. "The powers of the gods are not meant for humans to trifle with. I hope our paths cross again in this sacred space," Ashwatthama expresses, rising from his seat.

Eka's eyes reflect his earnest desire as he pleads, "Can you take me with you?"

Ashwatthama's brows furrow inquisitively. "Why?" he asks, curious about Eka's request.

"To learn more about this world," Eka responds, his thirst for knowledge evident.

Ashwatthama pauses, considering Eka's plea. "There is still time, my friend," he replies thoughtfully. "And time is all you have until my curse is revoked. Until then, I walk alone," he adds, alluding to his own eternal solitude as imposed by Shri Krishna's curse.

"I can't wait to meet you again," Eka says with anticipation. "I hope the next hundred years bring experiences as intriguing as they are unpredictable, unlike the blandness of the prasad," he remarks, expressing his hope for the future.

With a respectful nod, Eka seeks Ashwatthama's blessing as Ashwatthama prepares to depart from the temple grounds.

□

Chapter 18

Bharat 1523 A.D. – The Invaders

The Present

"Dad, can I have some chocolate?" Omkar requested, his eyes wide with hope.

"No way," Eka replied firmly.

The old man, standing nearby, looked worried. He pleaded silently with Eka, not to say a word.

"Why do I have to eat the same hospital food and medicine when Eka couldn't eat the same prasad?" Omkar asked, puzzled.

"Eka's is centuries old," Eka explained gently.

"But I'm ten years old! How can you compare him with me? Wouldn't Eka transfer a hundred years of his life to me in a jiffy?" Omkar asked, his innocence shining through.

Eka was taken aback by the child's wisdom. "I'm sure he would. He wouldn't even think for a second," Eka said, feeling a swell of love for his son. He hugged him tightly. "Let me get your chocolate," he added, a smile spreading across his face.

Omkar grins at his grandfather. The old man stepped forward, handing him the chocolate with a warm smile.

Ashwatthama strides forward with renewed vigour, his demeanour transformed. His once worn-out appearance now radiates vitality. The scars and boils that marred his skin have faded, replaced by a healthy glow. Clad in fresh attire, he exudes a youthful aura, a stark contrast to his former wanderer's guise.

As he traverses the unfamiliar terrain, Ashwatthama's gaze sweeps the surroundings in search of the temple. Yet, the once bustling area now appears desolate, devoid of the lively presence he once knew. Approaching a frail couple amidst the altered landscape, he inquires about the location of the Shiva temple, eliciting only fearful stares in response. With a wordless gesture, the woman points towards the east, prompting Ashwatthama to offer his gratitude before proceeding in that direction.

Upon reaching the temple grounds, Ashwatthama is met with a scene of desolation. The majestic Nandi statue lies damaged, a testament to the temple's state of ruin. The once magnificent edifice now stands dilapidated, its walls bearing scars from past assaults, its sacred artifacts defiled. In the absence of any signs of life, an eerie silence pervades the air.

Approaching the Janvapi pool, Ashwatthama observes its stagnant, blackened waters, a stark contrast to the vibrant pool he once knew. Ascending the temple steps, he encounters a different lingam, its presence indicative of the temple's altered state. Inside, the interiors bear little resemblance to their former glory, a poignant reminder of the passage of time and the temple's decline.

Seated before the forlorn structure, a solitary priest catches Ashwatthama's eye. As he engages in prayer, the priest regards him with surprise before hastily preparing prasad, a gesture of hospitality to the lone visitor.

"Have some prasad, O monk. You are the first visitor in a week," the priest offers, presenting a humble offering of grated coconut with sugar.

Curious about the temple's plight, Ashwatthama queries the priest about the grim state of affairs.

"The invaders ransacked the temple twenty years ago, threatening death to any who dared to approach," the priest reveals, recounting the tragic events.

Concerned for the fate of his friend, Ashwatthama seeks information about his former king, Ekanayaka.

"What happened to your king, Ekanayaka?" he asks.

"The invaders slew him after his valiant defence of the temple," the priest somberly informs him, shedding light on the tragic end of a noble ruler.

Suddenly, their tranquil moment is disrupted by the sight of a beggar charging towards them. The beggar's appearance is disheveled, with long, unkempt hair cascading over his shoulders. His clothes are tattered and soiled, bearing the marks of a life spent on the streets. His face, weathered by hardship, bears the lines of countless struggles, and his eyes reflect a mixture of desperation and longing.

"Get out of here!" the priest shouts, moving to shoo the beggar away, but Ashwatthama intervenes, recognising the beggar as Eka. He holds Eka back, much to the shock of the priest.

"He is with me," Ashwatthama assures the priest, asserting his authority.

Eka snatches the prasad from Ashwatthama and begins devouring it without a word. His silence is unnerving, and the priest looks on in stunned disbelief as Eka continues to eat voraciously.

Eka approaches the idol and notices some broken coconut pieces nearby. Without hesitation, he picks up the fallen fragments and begins to consume them hungrily, his actions driven by a primal need.

"Kindly get some food for my friend, sir," Ashwatthama requests the priest, his voice tinged with concern as he gestures towards Eka, who continues to eat in silence, seemingly oblivious to his surroundings.

Observing his friend's silent anguish, Ashwatthama motions to the priest, "Kindly get some food for my friend, sir."

The priest, still taken aback by the unexpected turn of events, nods silently and hurries off to fulfill the request.

As Eka finishes his meal, he collapses at Ashwatthama's feet, tears streaming down his face. Ashwatthama gently lifts him up, offering comfort in his embrace.

"Get up, Eka," he urges softly, his voice filled with compassion.

Eka rises slowly, his eyes brimming with emotion. "Look what they have done to my temple," he cries, his voice trembling with sorrow.

Concerned, Ashwatthama consoles him, "What happened, Eka?"

"We knew there were invaders, hell-bent on destroying

our culture and looting our temples, marching towards us," Eka begins, his tone grave with the weight of impending conflict. "I sent my armies to the north to defend our borders."

Ashwatthama listens intently, his curiosity piqued. "You weren't with your army?" he asks, seeking clarification.

"I was, but I had to return back to celebrate Maha Shiva Ratri in the kingdom," Eka responds, a hint of reverence in his voice.

"Why would you leave the army and come back?" Ashwatthama questions, intrigued by Eka's decision.

"Is there anything greater in this world than Shiva?" Eka counters, his faith unwavering.

"Then what happened?" Ashwatthama prompts, eager to hear the rest of the story.

"On the day of Maha Shiva Rathri, the air was charged with anticipation as I rose before dawn, my heart filled with reverence. The first light of day found me at the river, where I immersed myself in the purifying waters, performing ablutions to cleanse body and soul. With each splash of water, I felt the weight of the world washing away, leaving me renewed and ready for the sacred rituals ahead.

As the sun began its ascent, I made my way to the temple, where a vibrant scene greeted me. The temple grounds were alive with activity, bustling with devotees from far and wide who had gathered to pay homage to Lord Shiva. The air was heavy with the sweet scent of incense, mingling with the earthy aroma of freshly bloomed flowers, creating an atmosphere of divine sanctity.

Streams of pilgrims flowed in like rivers converging towards a sacred confluence, each one bearing offerings of milk, yogurt, honey, ghee, sugar, and water – symbols of devotion and surrender to the divine. The temple courtyard echoed with the sounds of chanting and prayers, a melodic symphony that rose and fell like the rhythmic pulse of the universe itself.

As the day progressed into night, the fervour only intensified. The temple became a beacon of light amidst the darkness, drawing devotees like moths to a flame. Yet, despite the throngs of people, there was an underlying sense of tranquility and serenity that enveloped the sacred space.

Amidst this sea of humanity, I found myself drawn to the central sanctum, where the divine presence of Lord Shiva awaited. With reverence in my heart, I offered my prayers and performed the Tandava Nritya–the cosmic dance of creation, preservation, and destruction. In that moment, I felt myself becoming one with the rhythm of the universe, swept away by the divine ecstasy of devotion.

As the night wore on, the temple remained aglow with the light of countless oil lamps, illuminating the path of spiritual seekers on their journey towards enlightenment. And amidst it all, I found myself filled with a profound sense of peace and contentment, knowing that I was in the presence of the divine." Eka tells it to a seriously listening Ashwatthama.

"Now we fast and pray in the temple till the morning," Eka announces solemnly, his voice carrying through the temple grounds with a sense of authority and devotion.

As he speaks, Eka is flanked by a procession of priests, locals, and a handful of guards, all drawn together by the shared reverence for Lord Shiva. Their footsteps echo softly against the temple's stone floors as they move in unison towards the sanctum.

Inside the temple, the air is thick with the scent of incense and the flickering light of oil lamps casts a warm glow upon the gathered devotees. The sacred mantra of Shiva, "Om Namah Shivaya," reverberates through the chamber, filling the space with divine vibrations.

Amidst the chanting, a special Puja is conducted, with offerings of fragrant incense and ghee-lit lamps made to the deity. Each gesture is performed with meticulous care and devotion, as the devotees lose themselves in the rhythm of the rituals.

Eka's voice trembled as he recounted the harrowing tale to Ashwatthama, his eyes haunted by the memories of that fateful day.

"That is when the outsiders came, disguised as locals and wandering saints," Eka began, his voice tinged with bitterness. "About 500 of them. They butchered everyone in their wake."

His fists clenched with barely contained fury as he continued, "I was escorted to the back of the temple with a few of the guards."

His words hung heavy in the air, each syllable weighted with the gravity of the events he described. "They broke open the temple door. We fought them bravely. But we were overwhelmed. I was stabbed multiple times. I fell to the floor."

The agony of that moment seemed to wash over him anew as he spoke, his voice strained with the pain of reliving the ordeal. "I lost all my men. But not before they dragged my body to the safety of the hidden room behind the temple. I could see the invaders desecrate the temple. But I couldn't do anything."

In the midst of chaos and destruction, an ominous presence materialised before Eka, unseen by the invaders who ravaged the sacred temple. Yama, the god of death, rode upon his black bull, his form looming over Eka with an otherworldly aura. The sight sent shivers down Eka's spine as he beheld the divine figure that only he could perceive.

Meanwhile, amidst the clamor of the invaders, their leader barked orders with ruthless efficiency. "Where is their king?" he demanded, his voice echoing with authority.

"We stabbed him. I am sure he is dead," another soldier asserted confidently, his words dripping with disdain for their fallen foe.

"Find the body and get me the head," the leader commanded, his tone brooking no dissent as he directed his men to search for their vanquished enemy.

With ruthless determination, the invaders turned their attention to the sacred lingam, intent on desecrating the very heart of the temple. But as they attempted to move the sacred stone, they found themselves thwarted by an unseen force, their efforts proving futile against its immovable weight.

"It must be stuck to the ground!" the soldier growled in frustration, his anger mounting as the lingam defied their attempts to defile it.

Undeterred by the obstacle, the soldier ordered the destruction of the sacred symbol, his command met with the sound of hammer striking stone. The hammer breaks. Eka watched helplessly, his heart heavy with despair as he longed to intervene but found himself weakened and unable to act.

In a moment of desperation, Eka reached for a vial concealed within his sword sheath, his trembling hands uncorking the container to reveal its deadly contents. With a resigned sense of defeat, he raised the vial to his lips and drank deeply, the bitter taste of poison burning his throat as it coursed through his veins.

As the lethal concoction took hold, Eka collapsed to the ground, his world spinning as darkness threatened to engulf him. Yet, in the midst of his despair, an unexpected turn of events unfolded before him.

Yama, the god of death, approached with his lasso in hand, ready to claim Eka's soul for the afterlife. But as the noose descended, a miraculous defiance occurred—Eka began to spit out the poison, his body rejecting the lethal substance with an inexplicable resilience.

Disappointed by his inability to claim Eka's life, Yama withdrew, leaving Eka to contemplate the inexplicable turn of events.

"But you know you wouldn't die," Ashwatthama interjected, his voice cutting through Eka's anguish with a tone of understanding.

Eka's eyes, heavy with sorrow, met Ashwatthama's gaze, the weight of his words hanging in the air like a solemn lament. "I lost everything," he murmured, his voice tinged with regret and pain. "I couldn't protect the things I loved. I was desperate to die."

"I woke up the next day to a scene of devastation," Eka recounted, his voice heavy with the weight of the memories. "The invaders couldn't break the lingam, so they shattered everything else in the temple."

His words carried the bitter taste of defeat, a stark reminder of the helplessness he had felt in the face of overwhelming odds. "I hid in the secret room for three days without food or water," he continued, his voice tinged with exhaustion. "I couldn't do anything. I was helpless. My throat burned with the taste of poison, but there was no relief to be found."

"On the third morning, when I was certain the invaders had left, I emerged from my hiding place," Eka revealed, the pain of his ordeal etched into his weary features. "I wept before the lingam, my heart heavy with sorrow and regret."

"I tried lifting the lingam, and to my surprise, I found that I could easily lift it," he said, a glimmer of hope entering his voice.

"As they say, faith can move mountains..."

Taking a deep breath, Eka continued his tale. "I changed into the clothes of a deceased priest, concealing the lingam with me as I made my escape," he recounted, his voice tinged with urgency. "I heard whispers among the people as I fled–rumours of betrayal and treachery, of a new king rising from the ashes of our defeat."

"And so, I went into hiding, living the next fifty years as a beggar," Eka concluded, his words heavy with the weight of his past. "But even in the shadows, I never forgot who I was or the price I had paid for survival."

"You know those soldiers can't kill you. Why didn't you attack them?" asked Ashwatthama, his voice filled with curiosity and concern.

"They can't kill me... but they killed my spirit the moment they broke my temple," replied Eka, his words heavy with the weight of his sorrow.

"You have so many other talents like hunting, building, warfare. Why did you choose to stay as a beggar for the last fifty years?" inquired Ashwatthama.

"I told you, I had a mission in this life, and that is to find *amrut*. Being a beggar helps me to travel without raising many doubts," replied Eka, determination shining in his eyes.

"I told you that is a wild goose chase. Why do you keep insisting on finding something which can't be found?" pressed Ashwa, his voice tinged with frustration.

"The day I lost my riches, the day I lost my kingdom, my temple, the people I loved, and I was forced to drink poison. You know what else happened on Mahashivratri?" asked Eka, a spark of revelation in his eyes.

"What?" questioned Ashwatthama, his interest piqued.

"Shiva gulped the Halahala produced during Samudra Manthan and beheld it in his neck, which was bruised and turned blue, after which he was named as Neel Kanth," Eka revealed, his voice filled with significance.

"So you and Shiva drank poison. It's just a mere coincidence," replied Ashwa, trying to make sense of the connection.

Eka then removed a robe covering his neck, revealing a

startling sight. His neck had turned blue, mirroring the divine manifestation of Shiva. Ashwatthama was shocked into silence, unable to find the words to express his astonishment.

"I believe I am destined to find the *amrut*," Eka declares with unwavering conviction, his eyes alight with determination as he gazes into the distance.

As if on cue, the temple priest arrives bearing a humble offering of food, which he presents to Eka with reverence.

"Is this a new lingam in the temple?" Eka inquires.

"Yes, the invaders destroyed the old lingam," the priest responds solemnly, his voice tinged with sorrow at the loss.

With a sense of purpose, Eka retrieves the old lingam from his bag, presenting it to the priest with a commanding presence. "This is the old lingam. Kindly replace the new lingam with this one," he instructs firmly, his words carrying an air of authority.

"Yes, and I am Lord Shiva... kindly pray to me," the priest retorts, a hint of skepticism evident in his tone.

"My friend has been through a lot. Kindly ignore him," Ashwatthama intervenes, seeking to defuse the tension and protect Eka's dignity.

Frustrated by the priest's lack of understanding, Eka turns to Ashwatthama with a mixture of disbelief and exasperation. "See these fools, Ashwatthama? They don't believe the truth... Fools are worshipping a stone when this is the real lingam," he declares, gesturing emphatically to the sacred object in his hand.

The priest, taken aback by Eka's fervour, regards him with a perplexed expression before quietly excusing himself from their presence.

"You seem to be hale and healthy. Your scars and boils have healed," Eka observes, his eyes scanning Ashwatthama's transformed appearance with a mixture of awe and curiosity.

"I roamed this world for 3,000 years. My curse has finally been lifted," Ashwatthama responds, his voice tinged with a sense of liberation as he reflects on his newfound freedom from the shackles of his past.

"What will you do now?" Eka inquires, eager to learn of Ashwatthama's plans for the future.

"The same thing I have done all this while... Roam the world and pray to Shiva at each and every Shiva temple," Ashwatthama declares with quiet resolve, his devotion to the divine unwavering.

"We both are Shiva bhakts... Why don't you help me in finding the *amrut*?" Eka proposes, his eyes alight with the prospect of embarking on a shared quest for the elixir of immortality.

Ashwatthama smiles knowingly, his expression conveying a sense of wisdom gained through millennia of existence. "Eka, there is no more *amrut* left... The Devas consumed it all," he reveals, punctuating his words with a note of finality.

"Then what did you give me that made me an immortal?" Eka questions, his brow furrowing in confusion as he grapples with the revelation.

"Some questions are better left unanswered," Ashwatthama remarks cryptically, rising to his feet with a sense of purpose.

"Please take me with you... I beg you... I wish to know the secrets of the world," Eka pleads, desperation evident in his voice as he implores Ashwatthama to grant him companionship on his journey.

"I can't take you, Eka... And some secrets are better off if they remain a secret," Ashwatthama asserts, his tone firm yet tinged with regret.

Undeterred, Eka makes a bold move, attempting to physically halt Ashwatthama's departure. "I am coming with you whether you like it or not," he declares defiantly, determination flashing in his eyes.

In a swift and unexpected motion, Ashwatthama pushes Eka away, his action fueled by a mixture of surprise and concern. "What are you doing, Eka?" he questions, his voice tinged with alarm as he watches Eka collide with a nearby tree.

As Eka struggles to regain his bearings, Ashwatthama offers a parting farewell, his words carrying a weight of finality. "See you in 100 years, my friend. 1623 to be precise," he states, before disappearing into the distance, leaving Eka to grapple with the profound implications of their encounter. Stunned by the display of Ashwatthama's power, Eka takes a deep breath, his mind racing with unanswered questions and unresolved emotions.

□

Chapter 19

Bharat 1623A.D. – Neelakantha

The Present

Omkar's shock reverberates through the hospital room, his voice trembling with disbelief and anguish as he struggles to comprehend the events that have unfolded.

"Why would Eka even put his hand on Ashwatthama? Ashwatthama is a god!" Omkar's cry echoes desperation and confusion.

In response, Eka offers a calm smile, his demeanour serene despite the chaos swirling around them. "You are forgetting, Eka too was once a god." with "You are forgetting that Eka was once a king, a bandit, and an immortal with a blue shade on his throat like Shiva, making him as powerful as a god." he replies, his tone carrying a subtle undertone of reassurance and self-assurance.

As Ashwatthama approaches the temple, he notices subtle improvements compared to what he witnessed a century ago. The once barren surroundings have regained their lush greenery, and the Janvapi well appears cleaner, hinting at a gradual restoration of the area. However, remnants of the past events still linger, evident in the broken statues and the somber atmosphere around the temple.

Amidst this scene, Ashwatthama spots Eka, clad in vibrant robes reminiscent of a voodoo doctor, adorned with white viboothi markings, and leaning on a walking stick. His attire exudes an aura of mystique and wisdom.

"Looks like you've had an eventful century," Ashwatthama remarks, acknowledging Eka's striking appearance.

"Let us pray first, my friend," Eka suggests, leading Ashwatthama to join the queue for worship at the lingam.

As they engage in prayer, Ashwatthama is surprised by the curious glances cast towards Eka's attire, marking him as someone distinct amidst the worshippers. After their prayers, they find a quiet spot near the Janvapi pond to converse.

Suddenly, Eka presents Ashwatthama with a peculiar fruit resembling human hands.

"Try this," Eka urges, offering the unusual fruit.

Perplexed, Ashwatthama accepts the fruit and takes a tentative bite.

"It tastes like an orange," he comments, surprised by its flavour.

"It's called Buddha's Hand, a citron found in the forests surrounding my tribe. It has no fruit, pulp, seeds, or juice, only sweet rind," Eka explains, shedding light on the unique fruit's origins.

Intrigued, Ashwatthama takes another bite, savouring the unusual delicacy as Eka shares more about his current pursuits.

"I am now a shaman living among the tribes," Eka reveals, prompting Ashwatthama's curiosity.

"How did you end up there?" Ashwatthama inquires, eager to learn more about Eka's journey.

Eka's voice resonates with a sense of adventure and determination as he recounts his quest for amruth, his words infused with an air of mystique and wonder.

"My quest for *amrut* led me on a journey across Bharat, a nomad traversing the vast expanse of our land," Eka begins, his voice tinged with a sense of wonder. "It was during my travels that I encountered whispers from seers, tales of a mystical herb said to thrive in the northern reaches of the Himalayan forests. The notion of *amrut* existing in the form of an herb was a revelation, shattering preconceived notions of its essence."

Pausing for a moment, Eka reflects on the unexpected twist in his quest. "For so long, I had only envisioned *amrut* as a liquid elixir, a potion of divine nectar bestowed upon the worthy," he continues. "To discover that it could manifest in the form of a herb was a revelation that ignited a fire of curiosity within me, driving me to seek out this elusive botanical marvel."

"In my pursuit of knowledge, I delved into the sacred texts, immersing myself in the timeless tales of our heritage," he recounts. "Among them, the Ramayana stood as a testament to our ancient lore, its verses holding clues to mysteries long forgotten."

"It was within the pages of the Ramayana that I uncovered the significance of the *Sanjeevani booti*," he reveals. "A herb of unparalleled potency, it was said to have been employed in times of dire need, long before the churning of amruth heralded its arrival."

Ashwatthama interjects with a question born of curiosity. "Could the seers have been referring to the legendary *Sanjeevani booti*, the very herb that saved Lakshman's life?"

Eka nods his head.

"According to the Ramayana, when Lakshman lay on the brink of death, Sushena, the physician of the Vanaras, imparted to Hanuman the knowledge of a miraculous herb, nestled within the cradle of the Himalayan peaks."

Ashwatthama listens intently, his mind drawn into the vivid imagery of the ancient epic. "With time dwindling and the fate of Lakshman hanging in the balance, Hanuman embarked on a perilous journey to the mountain, guided by the wisdom of Sushena," Eka continues, his voice carrying the weight of ages past.

"Yet, upon reaching the sacred mountain, Hanuman was met with a daunting challenge," Eka narrates.

"The mountain was cloaked in a tapestry of herbs, each one a testament to nature's bounty. Despite Sushena's guidance, the herb he sought eluded Hanuman's grasp, its identity lost amidst a sea of foliage."

"Sushena's years of training had honed his ability to discern the herb from its counterparts," Eka explains,

"And so, faced with the challenge of uncertainty, Hanuman resorted to an act of unparalleled courage," Eka continues, his words laden with awe for the hero's sacrifice. "With unwavering determination, he uprooted the entire peak of the mountain, carrying it back to the waiting Sushena, ensuring that no obstacle would hinder the revival of Lakshman."

"Hanuman acquired four herbs, each possessing remarkable properties," Eka elucidates, his words imbued with the weight of ancient knowledge.

"The first, Mrita Sanjivani, holds the power to resurrect the dead," Eka begins, his voice tinged with awe at the miraculous nature of the herb. "With its touch, life returns to those on the brink of departure, breathing vitality into the lifeless."

"Next is Vishalyakarani, a herb renowned for its dual capabilities," Eka continues, his tone resonating with reverence. "It not only extracts weapons embedded in flesh but also possesses the unique ability to heal wounds inflicted by these very weapons, restoring the body to wholeness."

"Suvarnakarani, the third herb, holds sway over the physical form," Eka elucidates, his voice carrying a note of admiration for its transformative powers. "With a mere touch, it can restore the body to its original complexion, erasing the scars of time and adversity."

"Lastly, there is Sandhani, a herb of unparalleled mending prowess," Eka concludes, his words painting a vivid picture of its capabilities. "It possesses the remarkable ability to join severed limbs and fractured bones, knitting together the fabric of the body with its mending touch."

"I journeyed from one place to another until I arrived at the tribe's settlement," Eka recounts, his voice carrying the weight of his odyssey. "When I reached them, I carried nothing but the essence of my being. Devoid of material possessions, I appeared before them as a humble wanderer. At first, they mistook me for a beggar, judging me by my outward appearance alone. However, upon beholding..." Here, Eka pauses, revealing his neck, now adorned with a vivid blue hue reminiscent of Neelakanta, "...they perceived me as a divine entity, a god who had descended upon them," he concludes, his words resonating with the profound impact of perception and belief.

"I assumed the guise of a deity, encircled by a throng of eager locals, hanging onto my every word with anticipation. They had congregated around me, yearning to hear the divine wisdom that their god would impart. And so, I began to narrate stories from our revered Vedas," explained Eka.

"Once, amidst a fierce battle, the Devas found themselves overpowered by the Asuras. In their desperation, they turned to King Muchukunda for aid. Without hesitation, King Muchukunda answered their call, engaging in a prolonged struggle against the Asuras.

In the absence of a capable leader among the Devas, King Muchukunda shielded them from the relentless assaults of the Asuras, persevering until they were able to find a worthy commander like Kartikeya, the valiant son of Shiva," recounted Eka.

"Then Indra said to King Muchukunda, 'O noble king, we, the deities, are indebted to you for your selfless assistance and protection, sacrificing your own familial joys. Here in the celestial abode, a single year equals three hundred and sixty years on earth. Much time has elapsed, and there are no traces of your kingdom or family, as they have been eroded by the sands of time. You arrived here in the Treta Yuga, and now it is the Dwapara Yuga on earth.'

'We are immensely pleased with you,' Indra continued, 'so please ask for any boon you desire, except Moksha (liberation), as that lies beyond our jurisdiction,'" Eka recounted.

"Muchukunda was overwhelmed with sorrow upon discovering the fate of his family, and although Moksha was the ultimate solace he sought besides reuniting with his loved ones, he realised it was an unattainable wish. Instead, he beseeched Indra for a boon to sleep, recognising that sleep might offer respite from his grief. During his battles alongside the gods, he had remained sleepless, consumed by his duties. Now, with his responsibilities fulfilled, exhaustion weighed heavily upon him, compelling him to seek rest."

"'O King of the Devas,' Muchukunda implored, 'grant me the ability to sleep. And let it be known that anyone who disturbs my slumber shall face immediate incineration.'"

"Indra consented, declaring, 'So be it. Go to the earth and find repose. Whoever dares to awaken you shall meet their end in flames,'" Eka narrated, his voice resonating with the gravity of the ancient tale.

"The locals were enthralled by my tales, especially the younger ones," Eka responded.

"Did they truly believe every story you told them?" inquired Ashwatthama.

“Absolutely,” Eka affirmed. “They regarded me as a deity, their chosen leader. Surprisingly, I didn’t have to engage in any battles to earn their respect. While they may have been considered primitive by some standards, they possessed remarkable longevity secrets. Unlike most who barely reached their sixties, these tribesmen often lived well into their hundreds.”

“They entrusted me with their most guarded secret,” Eka continued, producing a dried leaf from his belongings, which caught Ashwatthama’s attention.

“I believe you recognise this,” Eka remarked.

Ashwatthama nodded. “It’s the Sandhani leaf. I haven’t laid eyes on one in a millennium,” he said, struck by the rarity of the find.

“You’re right. I’ve utilised this herb to mend wounds inflicted by ferocious beasts—tigers and elephants alike. It truly is a remarkable herb.”

“I’m grateful for your efforts in aiding those in need,” Ashwatthama acknowledged warmly.

“Indeed, it’s a remarkable herb, but it’s not the one I seek,” Eka responded with a hint of disappointment.

“May you find what you’re searching for,” Ashwatthama offered a supportive sentiment.

“You know where to find it. Help me,” Eka implored, his tone becoming more urgent.

“I’m afraid I don’t understand what you’re referring to,” Ashwatthama confessed.

Frustration clouded Eka’s demeanour, reminiscent of his agitation a century ago. Abruptly, he rose from his seat and advanced towards Ashwatthama with intensity.

“Calm yourself, my friend. Let’s not let our meeting end on a sour note,” Ashwatthama urged gently, attempting to diffuse the tension.

“I apologise,” Eka relented, his demeanour softening. “I don’t know what came over me.”

“Until we meet again in a century, my friend,” Ashwatthama bid farewell, turning to leave.

“See you then,” Eka replied, watching Ashwatthama depart as they parted ways.

□

Chapter 20

India 1723 A.D. – The British Officer

The Present

Omkar's curiosity ignited like a flame, his eyes wide with excitement as he leaned forward.

"What is the sanjeevani booti?" he inquired eagerly, his voice laced with anticipation.

"It's a mystical herb said to possess the power to revive the dead and grant immortality," Mohan explained, his tone carrying a hint of wonder.

"Then why can't you give me sanjeevani booti?" Eka questioned, his voice tinged with frustration.

"I searched tirelessly for it, but alas, I couldn't find it," Eka admitted with a heavy heart, his disappointment palpable.

"But didn't the sages tell Eka that he would find it in the Himalayas?" Omkar interjected, his brow furrowing with confusion.

"And yet, the same fool had destroyed it," Eka lamented bitterly, his voice tinged with regret.

"But why?" Omkar pressed.

As Ashwatthama approached the temple, he was met with an unexpected sight. Battalions of British soldiers stood in disciplined formation, their vibrant red and black uniforms contrasting sharply with the surrounding landscape. Most of the soldiers were Indians, with only the officers bearing the unmistakable insignia of British authority. At a roadblock, the soldiers halted all civilians, but Ashwatthama was granted passage without question. "Good sire, the commander has been expecting you. Follow me," a British officer instructed, leading Ashwatthama towards the temple.

Despite the presence of foreign soldiers, the temple appeared unchanged from a century ago. The once barren surroundings had flourished into a vibrant greenery, while the Janvapi lake sparkled with newfound clarity, attracting a plethora of migratory birds. Amidst this scene, Ashwatthama observed some British officers engaged in an unfamiliar game.

Escorted to a tent pitched near the lake, Eka emerged, now dressed as a British officer. "Thank you, Sergeant. You may leave now," he dismissed the soldier with a nod.

"Ah, good friend, nice to finally see you," Eka greeted Ashwatthama warmly.

"Well, now this is a big U-turn. What happened?" Ashwatthama inquired, surprised by the unexpected turn of events.

"Have your prayers and get back. We will sit and talk," Eka responded cryptically, indicating that their conversation would have to wait until they were alone.

"Won't you join me for prayers?" Ashwatthama asked.

"Not in front of these gentlemen," Eka replied, his tone hinting at the necessity of discretion.

After completing his prayers in solitude, Ashwatthama returned to find the temple devoid of the usual congregation. He settled beside Eka at a table in front of the makeshift tent, where tea was promptly served.

"Why are you dressed as an invader? You told me you hated them," Ashwatthama questioned, eyeing Eka's British attire with a mixture of confusion and concern.

"Well, the British let me follow my own religion. Unlike the previous invaders, they don't force me to convert," Eka explained.

"Then why didn't you join me for prayers?" Ashwatthama probed further, searching for clarity in Eka's unexpected behaviour.

"They are jealous of my stature—my countrymen and the British alike. So, I am trying to blend in, to be like one of them. I follow my religion in private," Eka replied, his words laced with a touch of bitterness.

"What are you up to?" Ashwatthama asked, his curiosity piqued by Eka's enigmatic demeanour.

"I am an explorer for the British. It comes with many perks," Eka responded, as he nonchalantly placed a gun on the table.

"What is this?" asked Ashwatthama, his gaze fixed on the unfamiliar object in Eka's hand. He had never seen a gun before.

"One century's magic is another century's science," replied Eka, his tone reflecting a blend of reverence and pragmatism.

"This is the weapon of gods. This is the closest I have come to seeing a real Brahmastra. It stings like hell and can test any immortal. I've been shot thrice with this, and it's the maximum pain I have ever felt," Eka explained, his words laden with a sense of awe and discomfort.

As they conversed, an artist observed them from a distance, capturing their interaction on canvas.

Curious, Ashwatthama reached out and took the gun, examining it with a mixture of fascination and trepidation.

"I knew the Lord of Weapons would love this new weapon. Come with me. Let me show you how it works," Eka suggested, leading Ashwatthama to a target setup practice ring.

"I see a change in you, Eka," observed Ashwatthama, noting the shift in Eka's demeanour.

"Don't call me Eka. I am Eka the explorer," came the firm response from Eka, his identity now intertwined with his new role.

As Eka demonstrated how to load the gun, Ashwatthama couldn't help but reflect on the transformation his friend had undergone.

"You seemed so happy living with the tribes. What happened?" Ashwatthama inquired, his voice tinged with genuine concern.

"In every century, as people begin to notice that I do not age, I feel compelled to move on," Eka explained, his voice tinged with a hint of melancholy. "But here, among people who boasted long lifespans of 120-130 years, I felt a sense of belonging I had never experienced before. For the first time, I didn't feel like a freak; I was revered as their Shiva, their protector and guide."

Continuing his narrative, Eka revealed a dried leaf he had carefully preserved. "This is Suvarnakarani," he announced, his eyes reflecting a mix of reverence and regret. "I discovered it further north during my explorations."

With a thoughtful gaze, he continued, "I brought some plantations of Suvarnakarani back and began growing them near our tribe. The plant thrived in the pristine areas surrounding our settlement."

"I wanted to explore the properties of the plant," Eka admitted, his tone tinged with a sense of remorse. "According to the ancient texts written by Valmiki, Suvarnakarani has the ability to restore the body to its original complexion."

With a heavy sigh, he recounted, "Like a fool, I decided to test it on myself. Slowly but surely, the mark on my neck began to disappear, and the tribesmen began to believe that I was a charlatan posing as a god."

However, as time marched on, a subtle shift occurred in the perception of those around me. Initially, they marveled at my youthful appearance and apparent immortality, attributing it to some divine blessing or miraculous anomaly. Yet, as the years turned into centuries and my unchanging visage stood in stark contrast to the inevitable march of time, admiration turned to suspicion, and awe transformed into fear.

Whispers began to circulate among the community, fuelled by fear and uncertainty. They speculated that I must be siphoning away their life force to sustain my eternal youth, draining them of their vitality to fuel my own immortality. The once warm embrace of love and acceptance gradually gave way to the chill of distrust and suspicion, as my presence became a source of unease and apprehension among those who once welcomed me as a guardian and guide.

And so, I found myself isolated, a solitary figure amidst a community gripped by fear and mistrust, forever marked by the burden of my immortality.

"They finally hanged me, alongside the woman I had taken as my wife, in front of their tribe. She passed away within moments, succumbing to the merciless grip of death, while I endured the agonizing torment of hanging for a staggering 35 days. They stood guard, a constant reminder of my eternal suffering," says Eka, his voice heavy with the weight of past horrors.

"Do you know the ravenous hunger that gnaws at a man's insides when he is denied the solace of death, and his stomach remains empty for 35 excruciating days? I resorted to consuming the tiny ants and wriggling worms that dared to venture near my parched lips, a desperate attempt to quell the relentless ache of starvation," Eka questions, his gaze haunted by memories.

Ashwatthama listens in silence, his heart heavy with empathy for Eka's ordeal.

"The tribespeople, revelling in their cruelty, took aim with their arrows, using me as a target for their twisted amusement. I remained suspended from the tree, my body a battleground for the relentless assault of crows, eager to feast upon my sightless eyes, and voracious worms, seeking refuge within the confines of my nose," Eka continues, his voice trembling with emotion.

"When the bamboo holding my neck finally yielded, and I plummeted to the ground, my only thought was of sustenance. Amidst the chaos of my descent, I found myself surrounded by mushrooms, and without hesitation, I devoured them with an insatiable hunger. I lacked the strength to retaliate, too weakened by hunger and deprivation to muster a defense," says Eka, his words tinged with despair.

"Their belief in my reincarnation fuelled their relentless pursuit, driving me to flee for my life. I dared not endure another 35 days of agonising torment, dangling from the clutches of death. And so, with no other recourse, I plunged into the depths of a waterfall, mirroring the desperate act of survival I had undertaken millennia ago," concludes Eka, his voice trailing off as he relives the harrowing memories.

Thankfully, I was found by my British friends. They saved me from the clutches of death, and in return, they required someone familiar with the terrain. I became their guide, leading them to the territory of the tribes under the guise of promising great treasures," explains Eka, his tone laced with a mixture of relief and remorse.

"It was a devastating confrontation, pitting bows and arrows against the firepower of modern guns. The tribes, valiant but outmatched, faced a massacre at the hands of the British forces," Eka recounts, the weight of the memory evident in his voice.

"I obtained my revenge. To ensure their submission, I had to destroy the one thing that held value to them—their green gold, their precious Sandhani farms. We razed the fields to the ground, leaving behind a trail of destruction."

"As a result of my actions, I was rewarded, was recruited and as an official, explored with the British.

"Did you destroy all the Sandhani plants?" inquires Ashwatthama, his tone laced with curiosity and concern.

"Not all of them. I managed to salvage some, transporting them back to my own property. There, they are tended to by skilled gardeners, alongside the Suvarnakarani plants," responds Eka, his voice carrying a hint of reassurance.

As he speaks, Eka takes aim and fires a shot at a target, but the bullet veers off course, missing its mark.

"It's a work in progress. The precision of the aim still requires refinement," Eka admits.

Observing Eka's technique, Ashwatthama takes hold of the weapon and begins to replicate the steps he has witnessed—filling the gunpowder, loading the gun, and taking aim. As he works, he engages in conversation with Eka.

"I never imagined you to be such a spiteful man, Eka," Ashwatthama remarks.

"Times change, my friend," Eka replies.

"Why burn the Sandhani plantations? They could have been valuable for future generations," questions Ashwatthama, his brow furrowed in contemplation.

"Well, my friend, now is the future. In England, there's a demand for such plants. I can sell them to those white fools who are always entangled in wars," Eka responds, his tone tinged with a mixture of pragmatism and disdain.

"And what about the Sanjeevani plant? Did you manage to find it?" queries Ashwatthama, his curiosity piqued.

"I am confident I will find it. I know someone who possesses knowledge of its whereabouts," Eka reassures.

Ashwatthama steadies his aim and releases the trigger, the bullet finding its mark with precision, hitting the bullseye with a satisfying thud.

"The weapon performs admirably. It's essentially just an advanced version of the bow and arrow," he remarks, his voice carrying a note of approval.

Placing the gun back on the table, he turns to Eka with a solemn expression. "I'll see you in 1823, Eka. Hopefully, by then, you'll have found a better path than the one I see before me now," he says, his words laced with a hint of concern for his friend's journey.

Eka nods in acknowledgment, offering Ashwatthama the gun as a parting gift. "Take the gun with you. You never know when it might come in handy," he suggests, extending the offer of protection.

In response, Ashwatthama reveals the sword sheath hidden within his bag. "This sword hasn't failed me yet, and I trust it will serve me well in the future," he states confidently.

Eka's curiosity is piqued. "I've seen your sword, but what about your legendary bow and arrows?" he inquires.

Ashwatthama offers a knowing smile. "A bow and arrow draw too much attention. They're safely hidden away in a place where they'll remain undisturbed," he explains, leaving a sense of mystery lingering in the air.

As Ashwatthama begins to depart, he pauses, turning back to Eka with a curious expression etched on his face.

"What name do you go by now?" he inquires.

"I am known as Ekagra, but to the British, I am called John," Eka responds with a hint of resignation in his voice.

Ashwatthama furrows his brow. "That doesn't quite add up," he remarks.

"Nothing truly does make sense when it comes to the British," Eka replies with a wry smile, acknowledging the complexities of their interactions.

With that, Ashwatthama bids farewell and departs, leaving Eka to watch him go.

Eka summons his men, two young individuals in their twenties, who promptly stand before him.

"Follow that hermit and meticulously map out his travels. Report back to me once your task is complete," he orders with authority.

The men salute in acknowledgment before swiftly making their exit to carry out their assigned duty.

Meanwhile, the painter arrives with a finished portrait capturing Eka and Ashwatthama seated at the table.

"Document this and store it in the archives. I will have need of it in a century's time," Eka instructs the painter.

Though initially puzzled, the painter nods in compliance.

□

Chapter 21

Bharat 1823 A.D. – Search for the Sanjeevani

The Present

"Why did Eka destroy the plantations? They could have been beneficial to me and many others now," queries Omkar with genuine curiosity.

"He was naive in his youth. As he grew older, he must have come to realise that he shouldn't have made such a decision," explains Mohan.

"It's a story as old as time. A young person thinks, 'I wish old people were as wise and enlightened as I am.' But as that young person grows old, they reflect, 'I wish I had known how naive and ignorant I was when I was young.' I'm certain Eka must have recognised his mistake. However, fortunately, he has preserved many of them on his property," Eka replies, reflecting on the passage of time and the wisdom it brings.

As Ashwatthama walks towards the temple, he is greeted by a vastly transformed landscape. Lush plantations stretch out in every direction, meticulously tended to by numerous servants. The temple itself is a sight to behold, restored to its former splendour, with statues and the revered Nandi restored to their original glory.

Spotting Eka amidst this picturesque scene, Ashwatthama notices a marked sophistication in his demeanour. Dressed immaculately in all white, Eka pauses his game of badminton with two children and rushes to embrace Ashwatthama warmly.

"Carry on with the game," he instructs the children with a smile.

Shall we talk in the garden?" Eka suggests.

"I wish to pray first," replies Ashwatthama.

"Wait for me; I'll join you shortly. Let me cleanse myself in the holy Janvapi and change into appropriate attire. I can't enter the temple in these sweaty clothes," Eka explains before taking a purifying dip in the sacred waters and donning traditional garments. Together, they enter the temple, which is bustling with crowds of devotees. Ashwatthama notices the lingam has been restored to its original form–the very same lingam the invaders had tried to destroy.

"Do you remember this lingam?" Eka asks Ashwathama.

"Of course, I do. How did you manage to retrieve it?" Ashwatthama inquires.

"I simply explained that the idol was discovered during the temple's restoration," Eka responds with a hint of amusement.

"So when you told the truth, no one believed you, but when you lied, everyone did?" Ashwatthama muses.

"Regardless, I'm pleased to see the crowds returning," Ashwatthama remarks.

"It took 200 years for people to start coming back to temples again," Eka observes with a tinge of nostalgia.

"I am surprised you joined me in the temple. A century ago, you were refusing to join me in prayer," Ashwatthama remarks, curious.

"I was working for the British then. I am my own master now," Eka responds confidently.

"I thought you were worried about being yourself in front of the white man," Ashwatthama probes further.

"I hate them," Eka admits bluntly.

"Then why do you work with them?" Ashwatthama questions, puzzled.

"Because they pay in gold," Eka replies matter-of-factly.

"What do you do?" Ashwatthama inquires, seeking clarity.

"I sell magic herbs to the white man," Eka reveals.

"I heard from the locals that the white man is looting our nation," Ashwatthama adds, concerned.

"That's because the white man lives on a barren island where nothing grows... so he has to loot other nations," Eka explains with a hint of disdain.

"You have been to the white man's island?" Ashwatthama asks, surprised.

"Yes, they wanted to grow the magic herbs on their island, but these plants only grow here," Eka confirms, pulling out a leaf to illustrate. "This is the Vishalyakarani leaf. It is capable of extracting weapons and healing all wounds inflicted by weapons," he explains, showing it to Ashwatthama, who doesn't react as expected.

"You aren't surprised looking at it," Eka observes.

"If my memory serves right, I remember using Vishalyakarani in battle," Ashwatthama recalls calmly.

In the vibrant garden, the air is filled with the joyful sounds of two young kids energetically playing badminton. Ashwatthama, intrigued by the unfamiliar sight, observes them with keen interest.

"What are they doing?" he asks, his curiosity sparked by the lively game of badminton unfolding before him.

Eka, noticing Ashwatthama's curiosity, steps forward to offer an explanation. "It's a game called Poona, introduced by the white man. Allow me to demonstrate how it's played," he says, his tone eager to share his knowledge. With patient enthusiasm, Eka guides Ashwatthama through the rules and techniques of the game.

"I thought you hated the white man, yet you seem to want to become like them," remarks Ashwa, noting the apparent contradiction.

"I am simply inspired by the way they enjoy life. I'm only adopting the enjoyable aspects," Eka explains.

Eka calls the kids playing badminton, and they eagerly approach.

"Meet my kids," he introduces them to Ashwatthama, two young girls aged 5 and 8. They exude a vibrant energy and innocence.

The kids greet Ashwatthama warmly, and he blesses them before they return to their game.

"Adopted kids?" inquires Ashwa.

"Yes, for now but eventually, I hope to have my own children," replies Eka, with a hint of longing in his voice.

"That's not possible. You don't have a fate line," Ashwatthama points out.

"With science, anything is possible in the future. Someday, we might even journey to the moon. You've seen how rapidly the field of science is advancing," Eka responds optimistically.

"And how does your science explain you?" Ashwatthama probes further.

"In typical human cases, waste accumulates, and the body slowly deteriorates. But in my case, there is perfect regeneration of cells and detoxification. Conceptually, I can live for eternity. The same applies to you," Eka explains scientifically.

Ashwatthama reaches out and picks up the plant from the table, examining it with a mix of fascination and nostalgia.

"Where did you find this? I haven't laid eyes on this plant in centuries," he remarks, his tone reflecting genuine intrigue.

Eka, with a sense of pride in his accomplishment, responds, "I possess the resources, manpower, and ancient knowledge from our holy texts to locate these plants. It's remarkable that three out of the four plants mentioned by Valmiki were discovered in the Himalayan region. This particular one doesn't even grow on my estate; I had to establish a plantation in the Himalayas specifically for Vishalyakarani."

"I'm pleased to see you dedicating yourself to such noble endeavours for the betterment of mankind. After the incident with the tribes, I must admit, I feared the worst from you. But you've surprised me," Ashwatthama acknowledges, his expression softening with genuine appreciation.

"They attacked my wife. That's why I took such drastic action...but looking back, I wonder if it was the right choice," Eka confesses, his voice tinged with remorse.

"Glad to see you've changed," Ashwatthama replies, offering a supportive nod.

Eka's eyes light up with determination. "I believe I can do more for mankind, especially if you lend your assistance," he implores.

"And what, pray tell, do you need from me?" Ashwatthama inquires, intrigued by Eka's plea.

"I need your help in finding the Sanjeevini plant," Eka appeals, his voice filled with urgency and hope.

"You're the expert on plants. Seeing the Vishalyakarani after a millennium fills me with confidence. If anyone can locate the Sanjeevini, it's you," Ashwatthama responds, offering his trust and support.

Eka pauses, grappling with the gravity of the task at hand. "I'm uncertain...the Sanjeevani is the rarest and most precious of the four plants. The gods may have concealed it for its value and to prevent it from falling into the wrong hands," he explains.

Ashwatthama smiles warmly, a glimmer of encouragement in his eyes. "I must take my leave now, my friend. Until we meet again in 1923. I wish you the best of luck on your quest," he says, bidding farewell with a sense of hope and camaraderie.

They embrace warmly, and as Ashwatthama departs, Eka's gaze lingers on his retreating figure.

Once he's certain Ashwatthama has left, Eka calls several soldiers to his side, and about 15 men promptly respond, saluting him in unison.

"Follow the monk discreetly and meticulously record his movements. Ensure he remains unaware of your surveillance," Eka instructs them with a sense of urgency.

The soldiers nod in understanding, their expressions reflecting a mixture of determination and curiosity. One of them ventures to question, "Why do we need so many soldiers to track a monk? Two of us should suffice."

Eka offers a knowing smile before revealing a detailed map. "This map was crafted by the last pair who undertook this mission, but it's only half complete."

His words evoke a sense of surprise among the soldiers as they digest the gravity of their task.

"I have full confidence that you will exceed their efforts.

Every three years, some of you will return with updated maps, while the others will remain to continue tracking the monk. Upon your return, you will be replaced by a fresh group of soldiers to continue the surveillance. Your families will be looked after during your absence," Eka assures them, his tone resolute

After handing them the map, Eka watches as they salute him and depart, ready to embark on their mission.

A painter approaches Eka, presenting him with a new painting of himself and Ashwatthama. Eka carefully scrutinises it, comparing it to a similar painting he received a century ago. Remarkably, both portrayals depict them unchanged by time.

"Document this painting and store it alongside its predecessor in the library. I'll have need of both in a hundred years' time," Eka instructs the painter.

The painter acknowledges his directive with a respectful nod.

□

Chapter 22

Bharat 1923 A.D. – The Betrayal

The Present

Omkar, intrigued by the discussion, leans forward with curiosity. "If no one has seen the plant for many millennia, how was Eka so confident he would find it?" he asks.

Mohan responds, "He wasn't certain. He simply placed his trust in the holy books and scriptures."

Eka interjects, countering Mohan's statement. "No, he had a deep conviction that he would discover them."

Perplexed, Omkar questions further, "Why was he so sure?"

"Because of the history of the plant," replies Eka cryptically.

"What is the history of the Sanjeevini plant?" asks the kid, eager to learn more.

"After being tricked by Lord Vishnu, and losing the entire amrit to devas, the Asura Guru Shukracharya, greatest devotee of Shiva, feels remorse for the Asuras. He approaches God Shiva for justice, knowing that Shiva treats all beings equally," Eka explains.

Shukracharya beseeches Shiva, 'Hey Mahadev! Asuras have been cheated, and I fear their extinction. Please bless me with a mantra that would make the asuras invincible.'

Shiva replies solemnly, 'I will grant your request, but you must observe rigorous penance for a thousand years.'

With unwavering determination, Shukracharya embarks on his thousand-year penance.

"Upon completing his penance, Shiva, pleased with Shukracharya's dedication, grants him darshan and imparts the knowledge of Sanjeevani Vidya—the ability to bring the dead back to life," Eka continues.

"After acquiring this profound knowledge, Shukracharya transforms it into a herb and plants it in the Himalayas. Thus, the Sanjeevani Herb, which later saved the life of Lakshmana in the Ramayana, came into existence," concludes Eka.

Eka's son, Omkar, listens intently as Eka shares his insights. "This is just a story from our mythology," Omkar remarks.

Eka responds thoughtfully, "My son, the word 'mythology' is overrated. The truth is often simple. I found three out of the four plants that Valmiki mentioned. Sanjeevani is the last one."

Omkar's curiosity piques, and he queries, "Is that why he sent people to follow Ashwatthama?"

Eka nods in affirmation, acknowledging Omkar's astute observation. "But why is he so sure he would find Sanjeevini by following Ashwatthama? Ashwatthama told me he hasn't seen the plant in years," Omkar adds, seeking further clarification.

"The story is not yet over. Let me finish the story," Eka responds, his tone laden with intrigue, leaving Omkar eagerly awaiting the continuation.

"I have another doubt," Omkar begins, but his grandfather, Mohan, interjects gently, "Take your medicine now. Your father will clarify your doubts after you take your medicine."

As Ashwathama makes his way towards the temple, he can't help but notice the stark transformation of the surrounding landscape. What once was lush greenery now resembles an industrial area, with roads cutting through the foliage and small warehouses encroaching upon the once verdant space.

Reaching the temple, Ashwathama is struck by its dilapidated appearance. Its walls show signs of neglect, and the air is heavy with an aura of abandonment. Few people mill about, their presence echoing the temple's desolate state.

Amidst this sombre scene, Eka enters the temple, dressed inconspicuously like any other visitor. After exchanging greetings, they find solace in praying together within the temple's walls, though the absence of devotees is conspicuous.

"Where are all the devotees?" Ashwatthama inquires.

"Most of them have left the town," Eka responds solemnly.

Why?" inquires Ashwatthama, puzzled by the deserted atmosphere.

"The pollution has wrought havoc on everything here," Eka laments. "Even the lake is a victim. People have been dumping neel (indigo) into its waters, disrupting the ecosystem. Birds have ceased their visits, and the fish population has dwindled. The soil has turned infertile, hindering plant growth, and animals struggle to find sustenance. It's led to a mass exodus of people from the area. Even my own hair has begun to show signs of stress," Eka explains with a tinge of sorrow

Curious, Ashwatthama inquiries about Eka's change in fortunes since their last meeting. "What happened to you? You were flourishing when we last met."

Eka's expression darkens as he recounts, "The East India Company happened. Under British rule, we were compelled to cultivate indigo on a portion of our land as per their laws."

Astounded, Ashwatthama questions, "How could they force you to grow something against your will?"

Neel (indigo) being a cash crop which needed high amounts of water and usually left the soil infertile, we usually opposed its cultivation, instead preferring to grow daily need crops such as rice and pulses. "However, they enacted a new law that forced us to grow indigo." replies Eka.

Ashwatthama expresses concern, asking Eka about the fate of his plants.

Eka sighs heavily before responding, "Neel (indigo) cultivation rendered the soil infertile. As soon as I began growing neel, other plants started withering away. Despite my efforts to revive them, they simply perished."

Ashwatthama furrows his brow in confusion. "But wasn't neel in high demand? Didn't you earn money from it?"

Eka's expression turns grim as he explains, "The Germans developed a cheaper artificial dye, causing the demand for indigo to plummet. Now, all the crops have been left to ruin, and the indigo waste is being dumped into the lake."

Ashwatthama appears perplexed by Eka's mention of the ongoing world war.

"You're aware the world is engulfed in war," Eka states.

"I have fought in the Mahabharatha, the greatest battle ever witnessed. I no longer harbour interest or curiosity in wars," responds Ashwatthama with a sense of detachment.

"You're fortunate not to be affected by the turmoil around you," remarks Eka.

"The land, the temple, and the lake belong to you?" Ashwatthama inquires.

"No, they don't. The East India Company demands documents to prove ownership. Such formalities were never required before. The land was bestowed upon me by the kings," Eka clarifies.

Ashwatthama walks toward an inscription on the temple. Though damaged, the epitaph remains legible:

"Dedicated to Lord Shiva, built by Ekagraha Aahuk."

Ashwatthama's curiosity sparks as he questions, "You can prove that Ekagraha Aahuk was your ancestor, right?"

With a knowing smile, Eka searches his pockets and produces a document. It's a British-issued passport. "My official name is Eka John," he reveals.

Ashwatthama appears perplexed. "The British couldn't pronounce your name?" he asks.

"They may rule half the world, but struggle with a simple name," Eka remarks wryly.

"But until I provide them with proof, all these lands, the temple, and the lake belong to the British East India Company. You once told me, 'Hard times create strong men. Strong men create good times. Good times create weak men. And, weak men create hard times.' You were absolutely right," Eka laments.

"What will you do now?" Ashwatthama inquires.

"I will fight for our nation's freedom. I'm inspired by Subhash Chandra Bose. He aims to initiate an armed rebellion against the British. I've been a man of violence all my life, but at least now, I'll make my violence count," Eka declares with determination.

Ashwatthama acknowledges, "I've heard about him. Seems like a great man."

"After Jallianwala Bagh, people are growing more discontent with the British. It's only a matter of time before we gain independence," Ashwatthama predicts.

"Okay, friend, I have to leave," Ashwatthama announces, preparing to depart.

They share a heartfelt hug, and Eka ventures, "Can I come with you?"

"I travel alone, Eka. You know that. See you in 2023, my friend," Ashwatthama responds with a sense of finality.

"Hopefully, we will be an independent nation by then," Eka replies optimistically.

After Ashwatthama leaves, Eka unfurls the paintings he commissioned during his prior meetings with Ashwatthama., examining them closely. With a determined gleam in his eye, he strides purposefully to a local market bustling with the humdrum of daily life.

"I have seen God! I have seen God!" he exclaims, his voice cutting through the mundane chatter, drawing the attention of the passersby. Curious faces turn towards him as he proudly displays the drawings.

"My great-grandfather met the same man a hundred years ago. His great-grandfather encountered him two centuries ago. And now, I have just crossed paths with this divine figure in the Shiva temple," he proclaims, pointing at Ashwatthama in the images.

The crowd erupts into a frenzy, fuelled by Eka's fervent declaration. "Go that way! You'll find the god dressed in saffron robes. He is tall; you can't miss him. Seek his blessings." he directs them, indicating a direction with a commanding gesture.

As the crowd rushes off in pursuit of the supposed deity, Eka takes a moment to himself. Amidst the bustling market, he silently opens the meticulously charted maps detailing Ashwatthama's travels.

"Bless me, O Shiva, if Ashwatthama doesn't wish to take me with him. So be it... But I am determined to follow in his footsteps, whether he approves or not," he murmurs fervently, offering his prayer as he gazes towards the temple, his resolve unwavering.

Ashwatthama finds himself traversing a path, sensing the curious gazes and murmurs of the people around him. Their whispers gradually evolve into a following, causing him to quicken his pace. Yet, despite his efforts to evade them, the crowd persists, their numbers growing with each step he takes.

Soon, he is engulfed by a throng of individuals, each clamouring for his attention and seeking his blessings. They address him with reverence, hailing him as a deity and pouring out their grievances and hopes before him.

"I am not a god. I am just a monk. Please, leave me be," Ashwathama pleads, attempting to disperse the gathering.

However, his appeals fall on deaf ears as the crowd swells further, undeterred by his protests. The commotion attracts the attention of nearby British soldiers stationed at a checkpoint.

"Find out what's happening over there!" commands the officer, prompting the soldiers to intervene.

Ashwathama is intercepted by the soldiers, yet the people surrounding him express their indignation at the interruption, vehemently urging the soldiers to release him.

"Show your passport," demands one of the soldiers, seeking identification from Ashwathama.

The crowd vehemently opposes the soldiers' demands, insisting that Ashwathama, being a divine figure, is exempt from such formalities.

"What is your name?" questions the soldier persistently, attempting to ascertain Ashwathama's identity.

However, before Ashwathama can respond, the officer intervenes with a dismissive tone.

"His name is inconsequential. He could be Bhagat Singh in disguise for all we know. Arrest him!" the officer commands.

As the soldiers advance to apprehend Ashwathama, they are

obstructed by the impassioned crowd, who vehemently block their path. Tensions escalate, and suddenly, a gunshot echoes through the air as the officer fires a warning shot.

"Back away! You dont want to witness another Jallianwala Bagh massacre here!" the officer bellows, his voice tinged with authority.

The crowd steps back allowing the soldiers to proceed with their investigation. The officer orders a thorough search of Ashwathama's belongings.

"Check his bag!" he commands, prompting a soldier to inspect Ashwathama's possessions.

In a swift motion, Ashwathama pushes the soldier away, catching him off guard. The soldier stumbles backward, landing on the ground several meters away.

Enraged by the resistance, the British soldiers raise their weapons, aiming them at Ashwathama, who stands defiantly amidst the charged atmosphere.

Sensing the escalating danger, the officer takes drastic action, firing a shot at a random individual in the crowd, who collapses to the ground lifelessly. Ashwathama recoils, taking a step back as panic grips the crowd, sending them fleeing in all directions.

Satisfied with the display of power, the officer smirks. "Just as I thought," he remarks, his gaze fixed on Ashwathama.

The soldiers proceed to search Ashwathama's bag, discovering a sword within it. Intrigued by the weapon's ornate design, the officer surmises its potential origins.

"This appears to be of noble make. This beggar may have stolen it from royalty. Arrest him!" he orders, signalling for Ashwathama's detainment.

With Ashwathama in custody, Eka observes the unfolding events from a distance, his expression inscrutable as he contemplates the ramifications of the encounter.

□

Chapter 23
Har Har Mahadev

The Present

Omkar reclines on his bed, his mind buzzing with questions. "Why didn't Ashwatthama fight? He could have easily defeated the soldiers," he muses aloud.

Mohan, sitting nearby, offers a gentle smile. "He didn't want others to get hurt," he explains, his voice carrying a tone of understanding.

Perplexed by another aspect of the story, Omkar continues, "Why did Eka betray his friend?"

"Eka wanted to trail Ashwatthama. With a crowd surrounding Ashwatthama, his pace would have slowed, allowing Eka to follow discreetly without Ashwatthama noticing him"replies Eka.

"So Eka didn't anticipate the British arresting Ashwatthama?" Omkar inquires.

Eka affirms with a solemn nod, "Correct."

Curiosity still burning bright, the child poses another question, "Then why didn't he assist Ashwatthama?"

Eka sighs, explaining, "What could he do? He didnt have money to bribe the authorities."

"Then what did Eka's do?" asks the child.

"He pursued his long-held aspiration to trace Ashwatthama's journey, armed with the maps he held."

In the midst of heavy snowfall, the landscape transforms into a wintry wonderland. The roads, once bustling with activity, are now buried under thick layers of snow, rendering them impassable. Trees and rooftops are blanketed in pristine white, and icicles hang from branches and eaves, glistening in the soft light.

As Eka reaches the base of a hill, he encounters a man hurrying homeward through the snowy terrain. The man's breath forms misty clouds in the chilly air as he trudges through the snowdrifts.

"How do I reach the Shiva temple? Where is the path?" Eka inquires, hoping to continue his journey despite the harsh weather.

The stranger looks at him with a mix of concern and sympathy. "You can't go there," he replies solemnly. "The path is closed... It won't open for another 3 to 4 months, until the snow subsides."

Eka's heart sinks at the news, realising the magnitude of the natural obstacle before him. Refusing to yield to the harsh elements, Eka presses on, his determination propelling him up the snow-covered slopes towards the temple. Despite the treacherous conditions and the biting cold, he persists, following whatever semblance of a path he can discern amidst the wintry landscape.

Perched majestically upon the rugged mountainside, the temple Eka seeks holds a storied history and a profound spiritual significance. Known as the Tunganath temple, it stands as a testament to the enduring devotion of countless pilgrims who have traversed these mountainous trails in search of divine blessings. It holds the distinction of being the highest Shiva temple in the world, nestled at an elevation of over 3,600 metres.

Eka's memories of the temple are intertwined with the teachings of his guru, Adi Shankaracharya, with whom he once made the sacred journey to this revered site. Traditionally, access to the temple is limited to the months between June and October, when the weather is more favourable and the trails are clear of snow. Yet, despite the inhospitable conditions and the relentless blizzard swirling around him, Eka persists in his ascent.

As he finally reaches the temple, the solitude surrounding him is palpable. Normally bustling with pilgrims and devotees during the pilgrimage season, the temple now stands silent and deserted, its sanctity undisturbed by human presence.

For Eka, this moment serves as a poignant reminder of the resilience of faith and the enduring power of spiritual devotion. Despite the odds stacked against him, he stands before the Tunganath temple, a solitary figure amidst the swirling snow, his heart filled with reverence and gratitude for the opportunity to commune with the divine in this sacred sanctuary amidst the Himalayan peaks.

Upon entering the temple, Eka is enveloped by a profound sense of tranquility, finding solace amidst the flickering flames of the diya lamps that stubbornly defy the biting cold outside. Settling into a state of meditation, he immerses himself in the sacred space, his mind attuned to the divine presence that permeates the ancient walls.

As he reflects on the source of the illuminated lamps, Eka's gaze wanders, drawn to a solitary figure seated under a distant tree. Intrigued, he makes his way towards the sage, his footsteps echoing softly in the hallowed silence of the temple grounds.

Approaching the saint, Eka beholds a venerable figure lost in deep meditation, his countenance serene and his aura imbued with an aura of timeless wisdom. Beside him rests a bow and an axe, silent reminders of the sage's storied past.

In an instant, memories flood Eka's mind, recalling the fateful encounter with this enigmatic sage long ago. It was none other than the warrior saint Parashuram, whose formidable presence had once humbled Eka and reminded him of his mortal nature.

Moved by a profound sense of reverence and remorse, Eka prostrates himself before the immortal saint, his heart heavy with contrition for his past folly. "Forgive me, Maharaj," he implores, his voice laden with humility. "I was blessed to have encountered you once, a very long time ago. I was a fool then."

Parashuram, though silent, senses the sincerity of Eka's repentance. With a gentle nod, he acknowledges Eka's remorse before returning to his meditative trance, his form bathed in the ethereal glow of spiritual transcendence

Struggling against the weight of the heavy snowfall and the

encroaching darkness, Eka endeavours to find his way back from the temple. With each step, the snow becomes deeper, and the sky grows darker, making navigation nearly impossible. Realising the futility of his efforts, he reluctantly retraces his steps and seeks refuge once more within the temple's sanctuary.

Inside the temple, enveloped by the comforting aura of sacredness, Eka sinks to his knees and begins to pray. Time seems to lose its meaning as he surrenders himself to the rhythm of his devotions, his prayers merging with the silence of the night and the gentle flicker of the temple's lamps.

In the midst of his communion with the divine, Eka is startled by the unexpected presence of a priest.

"Bless me, Maharaj," Eka utters reverently as he bows before the priest, seeking his blessings.

With a gentle nod, Eka receives the priest's blessings.

"Eat the prasad, my son," the priest urges kindly, presenting the offering to Eka.

Accepting the prasad with reverence, Eka places it before the Shiva Lingam, honouring the deity's presence with the offering. "I will eat after Shiva has eaten," Eka responds respectfully.

Curious about Eka's presence amidst the raging storm, the priest inquires, "Why did you come amidst such a storm, my son?"

"For the blessing of Shiva, Maharaj," Eka responds respectfully to the priest's inquiry.

The priest's gentle smile reflects his reassurance. "His blessings are always with you," he affirms. "Spend the night here; there is too much snow, and you may lose your way down the mountains. The diyas will keep you warm."

Eka, intrigued by the priest's presence and his cryptic response, inquires, "Did you light the diyas?"

The priest remains silent, his enigmatic smile lingering, as he turns to leave. Eka, feeling a sense of urgency, calls out, "Where are you going, sir? You will get lost!"

As Eka rushes outside, hoping to catch the departing priest, he finds himself alone in the swirling snowfall. The priest has vanished, leaving behind a sense of mystery and wonder in his wake.

He awakens to the gentle light of morning, the storm now a distant memory. With a heart filled with gratitude, Eka offers his final prayers in the temple before beginning his descent down the hill. However, as he makes his way, he is astonished to encounter the same priest he had met just last night, approaching the temple from the opposite direction.

The priest's surprise matches Eka's own as he queries, "Dear son, where are you coming from?"

Eka, taken aback, responds, "From the temple."

Perplexed, the priest remarks, "The weather has been so severe these past months that even I couldn't go to the temple to light the lamps. How did you manage to reach there?"

Eka just smiles.

"The weather has just cleared. I am going to lock the temple until the weather improves."says the priest.

Concerned, Eka insists, "You better not lock the temple," and gives the priest some prasad.

As Eka continues his descent down the hill, a sense of revelation settles within him. He realises that it was none other than Lord Shiva himself who had manifested in the guise of the priest, bestowing his blessings upon Eka in a divine encounter.

□

Chapter 24

Jai Sree Ram

The Present

"Can I have your phone?" the kid asks Eka.

Eka gives him the phone, curious about what the child will do. The kid quickly opens the browser, searches for images of Lord Shiva, and then closes his eyes, praying earnestly.

Eka watches, intrigued. When the kid opens his eyes, Eka asks, "What did you ask the Lord?"

"Didn't you say we must not tell our wishes to others?" the kid replies with a wise smile.

Eka can't help but smile back. "You're right," he says.

"I prayed to Shiva to save me just as He has saved others," the kid admits softly.

"Don't worry," Eka assures him. "He is always with you."

Eka persists in his journey, diligently following the maps and retracing the paths once tread by Ashwatthama. His gaze is fixed predominantly on the Himalayas, recognizing them as the likely sanctuary for the elusive Sanjeevani plant.

Along his journey, Eka encounters landscapes that seem to defy earthly bounds. In the most remote and austere environments, he stumbles upon ancient Shiva temples nestled atop icy peaks and in desolate deserts. Despite the absence of human presence, the flames of the diya within these sacred spaces burn unwaveringly, casting their gentle glow amidst the solitude.

As he ventures deeper into these mystical realms, Eka encounters sages deeply immersed in meditation, their unwavering focus a testament to their spiritual dedication. Their serene presence amidst the rugged terrain serves as a reminder of the enduring power of devotion and inner peace.

Eka reverently encounters Kripa and Ved Vyasa deep in meditation at different locations in the Himalayas. With hands folded in respect, he offers prayers, hesitant to disturb their profound penance. Over the years of their intense meditation, nature has embraced them, intertwining trees and vines with their serene forms.

Venturing into the underground caves of Kerala, Eka encounters Mahabali, another chiranjeevi, or immortal being. Here, amidst the ancient darkness of the caves, Mahabali resides in contemplation, his presence evoking a sense of timelessness and spiritual power. Eka pays homage to Mahabali, acknowledging the enduring legacy of his benevolence and sacrifice in Hindu history.

In the sacred precincts of the Kedarnath shrine, Eka encounters a familiar sight—a child, devoutly praying near the Shiva idols, just as he had seen many times before in various locations. As he approaches the child, a realisation dawns upon him—it is Markandeya, the immortal sage known for his unwavering devotion and profound spiritual wisdom.

Filled with reverence, Eka humbly seeks blessings from Markandeya, recognising the divine presence that radiates from the young sage. In the hallowed ambiance of the shrine, amidst the timeless echoes of prayers and chants, Eka finds solace and inspiration in the divine encounter with Markandeya, a living embodiment of devotion and enlightenment.

Continuing his journey through uncharted territories guided by the maps, Eka encounters a daunting obstacle—a sheer icy cliff marking the apparent end of his path. Despite the maps insisting on pressing forward, the reality of the dead end looms ominously, presenting a perilous predicament.

With uncertainty clouding his mind, Eka surveys the desolate surroundings, finding no signs of life or guidance. Taking swift action, he erects a makeshift tent to weather the night, seeking respite from the biting cold and the weight of his dilemma.

As darkness envelops the landscape, Eka's rest is abruptly interrupted by ethereal hymns resonating through the stillness of the night. Intrigued, he ventures towards the source of the enchanting melody, drawn to a luminous green glow emanating from beneath the icy ledge.

Summoning his courage, Eka leaps from the edge, guided by an instinctual trust in the unseen forces at play. Landing safely on the ledge below, he finds himself standing before a cavern entrance suffused with the captivating radiance of the mysterious green light.

With each step into the cavern's depths, the hymns grow louder, echoing off the walls adorned with shimmering moss. Mesmerised by the otherworldly beauty surrounding him, Eka presses forward, drawn by an irresistible pull towards the heart of the cavern.

The hymns of "Jai Shree Ram" reverberate through the cavern, echoing with a divine resonance that sends shivers down Eka's spine. As he steps further into the immense chamber, he beholds a wondrous sight—a majestic figure seated in deep meditation: Hanuman, the embodiment of strength and devotion.

Overwhelmed by disbelief and awe, Eka trembles in the presence of the divine being he once deemed as mere mythology. In this frozen sanctum, surrounded by icy walls, the truth of ancient legends manifests before his very eyes, shattering the boundaries between myth and reality.

Within the embrace of the cavern, Hanuman is enveloped by the radiant presence of a sanjeevini tree, its ethereal glow illuminating the chamber with a celestial light. Moved by an inexplicable impulse, Eka approaches the tree silently, delicately plucking a single leaf and holding it in his trembling hand, a tangible relic of the miraculous encounter.

For a fleeting moment, the hymns cease, and Eka finds himself locked in a gaze with the divine Hanuman. Overwhelmed by a mixture of fear and reverence, he witnesses Hanuman resume his chanting, the rhythmic recitation filling the cavern with divine energy.

Caught in a whirlwind of emotions, Eka grapples with an urge to capture this surreal moment, to immortalise the incontrovertible proof of the divine's existence. Retrieving his camera from his bag, he hesitates, torn between the desire to share this transcendent experience with the world and the fear of desecrating the sanctity of the sacred encounter.

Setting up his camera amidst the divine chants of "Jai Shree Ram," Eka is bathed in the ethereal glow of the Sanjeevani tree, its luminous aura casting the cavern in a perfect light for photography. With trembling hands, he clicks the photo, capturing this surreal moment for posterity.

As the hymns abruptly cease, Eka peers into the camera's viewfinder, only to find Hanuman's piercing gaze fixed upon him. Startled, he instinctively averts his eyes, but when he looks again, Hanuman remains immersed in his sacred chant, his eyes closed in deep devotion.

Peering through the camera lens once more, Eka's heart races as he finds Hanuman's gaze locked onto him. Overwhelmed by fear, Eka watches in astonishment as Hanuman suddenly ascends upwards, the intense heat emanating from his divine presence melting the camera in an instant.

With a sense of urgency, Eka flees the scorching heat, scrambling out of the cavern and plunging into the icy waters below. Swimming frantically to the shore, he clambers onto solid ground, his heart pounding with the intensity of the encounter.

As he catches his breath, Eka retrieves the Sanjeevani leaf from his pocket, its once-glowing form now fading before his eyes. With a heavy heart, he watches as the leaf withers away, a poignant reminder of the fleeting nature of divine encounters.

Gazing skyward, Eka witnesses Hanuman's majestic departure, his form disappearing into the heavens above. Filled with a profound sense of reverence and gratitude, Eka offers a fervent prayer to Lord Hanuman, his soul forever touched by the divine presence he encountered in that sacred cavern.

□

Chapter 25

Bharat 2023 A.D. – Science and Technology

The Present

The kid smiles, and Eka is surprised.

"Why are you silent?" Eka asks.

The kid smiles again.

"You always say something or ask me a question about the story. Why aren't you talking?" Eka asks.

The kid is chanting softly.

"What's going on, Omkar?" Eka asks.

"I am chanting," Omkar says.

"Chanting what?" Eka asks.

"Jai Shree Ram," the kid replies.

Eka smiles warmly. "I am sure nothing is going to happen to you. Divine intervention is going to save you, Omkar," he says, hugging his child tightly.

Ashwatthama traverses the urban landscape, where concrete has usurped the once verdant greenery. Streets bustle with the ceaseless activity of shops and vehicles, the modern world starkly contrasting with Ashwa's timeless presence. Clad in contemporary attire—a shirt and pants—he navigates towards the temple, only to be confronted by a signboard proclaiming "Janvapi Mosque," a jarring sight that leaves him bewildered.

Approaching the familiar Nandi statue, Ashwatthama reaches out to touch its weathered form, seeking solace amidst the disheartening transformation. Where once a picturesque lake graced the surroundings, now stands a cluster of houses, devoid of any signs of life. The temple itself lies in ruins, its sacred space desecrated by the construction of a mosque, a grievous sight that pierces Ashwatthama's heart.

In this somber moment, Eka appears, extending a comforting greeting as they seek refuge under the shade of Nandi's watchful gaze. "Are you shocked, my friend?" Eka inquires, acknowledging the profound loss witnessed by Ashwatthama.

"It pains me to see one of the most revered temples of our time reduced to this state," Ashwatthama laments, his sorrow palpable.

Eka responds to Ashwatthama's observation about the temple's desecration with a disheartened sigh. "The court contends that there's no means to establish this as a temple, as the opposing party refuses to grant access for observers to conduct a survey," he explains, frustration evident in his voice.

"But surely, the structure's foundation alone speaks volumes about its sacred origins," Ashwatthama counters, his gaze fixed upon the remnants of the temple's architecture.

Eka nods in agreement, acknowledging the glaring evidence of the temple's sanctity. "Indeed, the foundation unmistakably denotes its religious significance. However, the legal complexities are compounded by the Places of Worship Act, 1991," he continues, his tone tinged with resignation. "This legislation prohibits the alteration of any place of worship and endeavours to preserve their religious essence as it stood on August 15, 1947."

With a heavy heart, Eka concludes, "Therefore, this legal dispute is poised to endure in the judicial system for a considerable duration, prolonging the temple's plight amidst the legal intricacies."

Ashwatthama's gaze sweeps over the barren landscape surrounding the temple, his expression a mix of sympathy and regret. "The complete disappearance of the greenery that once enveloped this temple is a tragic loss," he remarks solemnly. "Eka, my heart aches for you to witness the decline of your magnificent temple to such a state."

Eka acknowledges Ashwatthama's empathy with a sombre nod. "It is indeed a devastating sight," he concedes, his voice heavy with sorrow.

As they sit in the shadow of the Nandi statue, Eka shifts the conversation, his tone tinged with curiosity. "Nandiji has steadfastly awaited Shiva's return for a century," he observes, a glimmer of hope in his eyes. "Perhaps, like him, we too must endure this trial with patience and faith. Speaking of endurance, how did you find the last century?" he inquires, seeking to divert their thoughts from the temple's plight to broader matters.

Ashwatthama listens intently to Eka's account of his tumultuous century, his expression reflecting a mixture of sympathy and curiosity. "I have to say, this has been a terrible last 100 years," Ashwatthama begins, his voice heavy with the weight of his experiences. "I lost my sword and endured imprisonment until our nation gained independence. There were moments of misunderstanding, like when they mistook me for a soldier of Subhash Chandra Bose during a scuffle in prison. However, amidst the hardships, I had the privilege of meeting Bhagat Singh, which was perhaps the only silver lining in my time spent behind bars."

Eka listens attentively, his curiosity piqued by the mention of the legendary freedom fighter. "How was the great man Bhagat Singh? I only read about him; never had the chance to meet him," he inquires, eager to learn more about the iconic figure.

"After meeting him, I realised that some humans are at par with gods," Ashwatthama responds, his tone reverent as he recalls his encounter with Bhagat Singh.

Shifting the focus of the conversation, Ashwatthama turns to Eka, intrigued by his seemingly prosperous century. "How was your last century? You seem well off," he observes, noting Eka's apparent success and contentment.

Eka's face lights up with pride as he shares his achievements. "It was a fantastic 100 years. I am now the CEO of the world's biggest biotech firm," he begins, his voice brimming with satisfaction. "I started investing and buying lands from the government, where I grow medicinal plants like Vishalyakarani, Suvarnakarani, and

Sandhani. But the best part of it all is that I now have my own son," he adds, his pride evident in his words.

Ashwatthama's surprise is palpable as he processes the revelation. "An adopted son?" he asks, seeking clarification.

"No, my own blood and bones," Eka responds, his smile radiant with paternal pride.

"How?" Ashwatthama asks, his confusion evident.

"The advancements in science and technology, like cloning," replies Eka, his voice resonating with a sense of marvel and accomplishment.

"I am genuinely happy for you and your son, Eka. But what about your quest?" Ashwatthama inquires, redirecting the conversation to Eka's journey.

Eka pauses, momentarily puzzled by the question. "What quest?" he asks, seeking clarification.

"Finding Sanjeevani?" Ashwatthama reminds him, prompting Eka to recall his original mission.

"Ah, do you think I've reached my quest?" Eka questions, a hint of uncertainty colouring his tone.

"I don't believe so," says Ashwatthama, his voice tinged with reflection.

Curiosity sparks in Eka's eyes. "Why is that?" he asks, eager to understand Ashwatthama's perspective.

Ashwatthama's response is solemn, laden with the weight of observation and experience. "I couldn't reach Manasarovar or Mount Kailash as they are no longer part of Bharat. I needed a passport, which I don't possess... Why must I show this document to travel in my own land? Kashmir, once revered as the land of gods, has turned into a wasteland... I've witnessed the rapid destruction of natural resources, the extinction of rivers, animals, and birds... The disappearance of Ram Setu, Dwaraka and Saraswati. It feels like the Kaliyuga is upon us, and in such a painful world, Sanjeevani remains elusive," Ashwatthama concludes, his words heavy with the sorrow of witnessing environmental degradation.

Eka's smile held a knowing edge as he carefully opened a file, revealing the dry remains of a leaf nestled inside.

Ashwatthama's eyes widened in shock as he gazed at the leaf. "How did you get this?" he asked, his voice tinged with astonishment.

"How do you know what this is? You said you have never seen it before," Eka pointed out, his curiosity piqued by Ashwatthama's reaction.

"I have seen it in our scriptures," Ashwatthama replied, his tone indicating a mixture of recognition and disbelief.

"How many centuries will you lie to me, Ashwa?" Eka questioned, his words carrying a hint of accusation.

Taken aback by Eka's directness and the implications of his question, Ashwatthama paused, contemplating his response.

Then, Eka continued, his tone soft yet resolute, "Do you remember when you first visited my home? My parents slept outside, and they let you sleep inside the hut. That day, in the middle of the night while I prayed to Lord Shiva's drawing on our door, I saw your vessel glow in the dark. At first, I thought the vessel was reflecting light, but that night, there was only darkness. It was the Sanjeevani that was glowing in the vessel you carried."

"I am sure of it. I saw the same luminescence emit from the Sanjeevini plant in the cave where Lord Hanuman was praying. It's also written in the scriptures that Sanjeevani glows in the dark," he added, his conviction unwavering.

"You were carrying a live Sanjeevani plant with you when you came to my house. Even Sanjeevani-dipped water made me immortal. Imagine how many lives the plant can save," Eka continued, his voice resonating with awe and wonder.

"Where did you find the plant?" Ashwatthama asked, his curiosity now piqued.

Eka smiled as he took out a map. "I have tracked you with the help of my men for centuries. I have charted this map. I have met all the Chiranjeevis in my journeys. I have touched the Sanjeevani plant with my own hands but it was destroyed before I could retrieve it. Tell me, why do you hide your knowledge from me?" Eka asked, his gaze steady yet tinged with a hint of frustration.

In the annals of history, Banasura, a formidable asura, once reigned over a vast kingdom, instilling fear even in the hearts of celestial beings. As a devout follower of Shiva, he wielded his thousand arms to play the mridangam during Shiva's tandavam dance. When granted a boon by Shiva, Banasura sought his protection as the guardian of his city, rendering him invincible.

The Yadu army attacked Banasura in a great battle. When Lord Shiva was helping Banasura in his fight with Lord Krishna, Krishna and Shiva faced each other in battle. Krishna used a Brahmastra against Shiva's Brahmastra, a mountain weapon against a wind weapon, a rain weapon against a fire weapon, and his Narayanastra against Shiva's Pashupatastra. It was what the Westerners call a nuclear battle," says Ashwatthama.

"I was nearby during that cataclysmic battle, knowing the Sanjeevani herb would be imperiled. Hence, I procured some saplings, intending to transport them to safe havens in the Himalayas, away from human eyes. Seeking refuge in your father's home, an accident led those drops to fall into your mouth. Imagine the havoc and devastation humanity would wreak upon the world if they controlled the Sanjeevani," Ashwatthama explains.

"You're already a man of considerable wealth and power. How much more do you seek?" Ashwatthama questions.

"The herb isn't for me it's for my son. He is dying," Eka reveals, his voice tinged with urgency.

"Fate has already decreed that you cannot have offspring," Ashwatthama retorts.

"I write my own fate, Ashwa," Eka declares defiantly, his resolve unyielding.

Eka's voice carried a solemn weight as he spoke, "Even my father was told to let go of me, but he didn't. He hoped for a miracle, and a miracle happened. No father can see his son die."

"I am sorry, I can't let this knowledge fall into the wrong hands. We are already at the onset of Kali Yuga; Lord Vishnu will take his Kalki avatar and destroy the world. I am destined to be the Saptarishi, and I can't let humans interfere with the wills of God," replies Ashwattthama, his tone reflecting a sense of duty and inevitability.

"I just need a small plant, I swear I will use it only to save my son's life. Just tell me where I can find it," begs Eka, his desperation palpable.

"I am sorry I have to go now. I will see you in 2123 if the world isn't destroyed by then, and I will take these with me," says Ashwatthama, as he takes the maps and prepares to depart.

"The maps in my head and in my phone," he says, his tone light but with a hint of pride.

With a grin, Eka holds up his phone. "You have a phone, right? I will be damned if you don't have one," he remarks teasingly.

"You know I don't use such comfort devices" replies Ashwatthama, his demeanour reflecting a preference for simplicity.

"I roamed this world for 3,000 years. I feel this is the greatest man-made invention ever," Eka asserts, his admiration for technology evident.

Despite Eka's enthusiasm, Ashwatthama remains indifferent.

"Give me a hug, my friend... And be careful; this world has eyes everywhere... Especially with camera phones... You can't remain anonymous forever," Eka advises, offering a hug as he slips a small tag into Ashwa's pouch.

"Please, Eka, do not follow me or this time the consequences will not be pretty," warns Ashwatthama before departing.

Eka nods solemnly, understanding the gravity of the situation, and then checks his phone. The tag begins to beep on his phone.

□

Chapter 26

Battle of the Immortals

The Present

"That's it? Ashwatthama didn't give Eka the Sanjeevani!" Omkar exclaims, frustration evident in his voice.

"He will give it soon, don't worry. Take the medicine and have some rest. I will continue the story tomorrow," assures Eka, offering a comforting tone to the distressed Omkar.

He gestures for the old man to join him aside.

"Son, take care of him. You may be adopted, but I love you," Eka expresses warmly, his affection evident in his words.

The old man nods in understanding and then gestures towards the laptop.

"Ashwatthama has finally reached the parts of the map which I haven't charted. I am sure the Sanjeevani is somewhere there," Eka explains, excitement tinged in his voice.

"Do you want me to come with you?" asks Mohan, offering his support.

"No, no. Take care of my son. Track me if I am not reachable," Eka replies firmly, trusting Mohan to look after Omkar in his absence.

The old man nods solemnly, reciprocating Eka's hug before the determined explorer sets off on his quest once again.

Eka's helicopter touches down on a flat hilltop nestled deep within the majestic Himalayas. As soon as he steps onto the snow-covered ground, a fierce wind blasts against him, signaling the harsh conditions of the remote location.

Accompanying him are a squad of mercenaries, clad from head to toe in military-grade armour and armed to the teeth with advanced weaponry. The helicopter departs, leaving them alone in the wilderness.

Guided by his GPS tracker, Eka leads the group into a nearby cave, the entrance hidden amidst the rugged terrain. With cautious steps, they traverse the dark and icy passages, their progress illuminated by the glow of their fluorescent lights. Eka, carrying a bag containing essential supplies, maintains a determined stride as they delve deeper into the cavernous depths.

Eventually, they arrive at a spacious chamber within the cave, where vibrant green moss adorns the walls and floor, casting an otherworldly glow in the dim surroundings. The moss, thriving in the cold and darkness of the cave, creates an ethereal ambiance that captivates their senses.

"Switch off your lights," Eka whispers softly, signaling for them to extinguish their artificial illumination. As they comply, the cave is enveloped in darkness momentarily before the bio-luminescence of the moss fills the chamber with a mesmerising radiance, illuminating their path with a natural and mystical light.

With meticulous attention, Eka inspects every nook and corner of the cave, scouring through the icy chambers in search of the elusive Sanjeevani. The dim light of their torches casts eerie shadows against the frost-covered walls as they navigate through the labyrinthine passages. Each step echoes in the silence of the cave, heightening the suspense of the search.

After what feels like an eternity, Eka's keen eye finally spots a plant tucked away in a secluded alcove. His heart races with excitement as he recognises the telltale leaves of the Sanjeevani plant. Carefully, he approaches, his breath misting in the frigid air as he reaches out to touch the precious herb.

With trembling hands, he delicately uproots the plant, handling it with the utmost care to avoid damaging its delicate foliage. Cradling the Sanjeevani in his palms, he can scarcely contain his joy at the discovery.

With a sense of urgency tempered by caution, Eka carefully opens a small terrarium, its glass surface reflecting the dim light of the cave. Gingerly, he removes the Sanjeevani plant from its roots, handling it with utmost care to ensure its delicate foliage remains intact. As he transfers the plant into the terrarium, he can't help but feel a pang of anxiety, wondering if the transition will affect its luminous glow.

For a moment, he holds his breath, watching intently as the plant adjusts to its new environment. To his relief, the soft green glow persists, casting a gentle radiance within the confines of the terrarium. Eka's worry begins to ebb away as he realises the plant has adapted well to its surroundings.

"Take it and signal for the helicopter," he instructs one of the mercenaries, his voice firm but tinged with a hint of urgency. The mercenary nods in acknowledgment, accepting the terrarium with a solemn sense of responsibility.

Turning to the rest of the squad, Eka issues another directive. "The rest of you, continue the search for more specimens of the same plant," he commands, his tone leaving no room for hesitation. Each member of the team springs into action, their movements purposeful as they scour the cave in pursuit of additional Sanjeevani plants.

As the mercenary begins to depart with the precious terrarium cradled carefully in his grasp, a sudden, piercing pain courses through his body as an arrow finds its mark, lodging deeply into his flesh. Despite the agony, he maintains a tight grip on the terrarium, ensuring that his fall does not endanger the delicate plant housed within.

Amidst the chaos and confusion that ensues, all eyes turn towards the source of the unexpected attack. Emerging from the shadows with an air of regal authority and a demeanor that commands respect, Ashwatthama reveals himself in all his formidable glory. Clad in resplendent battle attire adorned with intricately crafted armour and wielding a bow of remarkable craftsmanship, he stands as a formidable figure amidst the dimly lit cavern.

His presence alone exudes an aura of power and strength, his steely gaze fixed upon the intruders with unwavering intensity. In that moment, it becomes evident that they stand before a warrior of legendary prowess, a figure steeped in myth and legend, now brought to life before their very eyes.

"Take your men and leave. I don't want to kill you, Eka," replies Ashwatthama with a solemn tone, his voice echoing through the cavern.

"I am unkillable, Ashwatthama, thanks to you. Put down your weapon and you will live," Eka retorts firmly, his words resounding with unwavering confidence.

Tension hangs heavy in the air as the mercenaries, poised and ready, await their next move. Ashwatthama, undeterred by the looming threat, closes his eyes in silent prayer, a serene calm enveloping him amidst the chaos. The mercenaries scoff at his gesture, their laughter filling the cavern with disdain.

But as Ashwatthama's eyes flicker open, a sudden transformation occurs. With a swift and practiced motion, he draws his bow and releases an arrow, its trajectory splitting into three distinct paths with remarkable precision. In an instant, three of the mercenaries are struck down, their cries of surprise and pain echoing through the chamber.

Amidst the cacophony of gunfire echoing through the cavern, Ashwatthama stands unscathed, the bullets of the mercenaries failing to penetrate his resilient form. With a steely determination, he retaliates swiftly, his arrows finding their marks with lethal precision, each strike incapacitating his adversaries with ruthless efficiency.

As the battle rages on, Ashwatthama remains unfazed by the onslaught, his focus unwavering as he systematically eliminates each threat. However, amidst the chaos, a sudden blow catches him off guard, a sharp jolt of pain piercing through his defenses. It is Eka, launching a relentless assault of punches in a brutal exchange of blows.

Their fists clash in a flurry of motion, the intensity of their fight escalating with each passing moment. Despite the ferocity of their confrontation, neither combatant succumbs to the pain, their bodies hardened by years of combat and resilience. Blow after blow is exchanged, the force of their strikes reverberating through the chamber as they engage in a primal struggle for dominance.

In the heat of battle, Eka's gaze falls upon a familiar sight amidst the chaos–a Sanjeevani plant, its presence a poignant reminder of his quest. With a momentary pause, Eka hesitates, his focus momentarily diverted by the unexpected discovery. Seizing the opportunity, Ashwatthama delivers a punishing blow to Eka's stomach, sending him reeling backwards with a gasp of pain. Eka collapses in a corner, blood staining his lips.

With a solemn expression, Ashwatthama retrieves his bow and arrow, a sense of resignation evident in his demeanour as he prepares for the inevitable. "I am sorry, my friend. I will truly miss you," he murmurs, his voice heavy with regret.

As Ashwatthama begins to chant a potent mantra, the air crackles with anticipation, the weight of their final confrontation hanging heavily in the air. With practiced precision, he notches an arrow onto his bow, his movements fluid and purposeful.

"You can't kill me. Your mantras can't kill me!" Eka's defiant roar echoes through the cavern, his unwavering resolve unyielding in the face of impending danger.

Undeterred, Ashwatthama's arrow ignites with an otherworldly flame, fuelled by the power of divine incantations. "I may not be able to kill you, but the astras of gods can," he intones, his voice resolute as he releases the arrow from his bow.

In an instant, the chamber is engulfed in a blinding blaze of light, accompanied by a deafening roar that reverberates through the depths of the cave. Ashwatthama shields his eyes from the brilliance, struggling to maintain his composure amidst the chaos.

As the brilliance fades, Ashwatthama's vision clears to reveal a shadowy figure emerging from the aftermath of the explosion. To his astonishment, there stands Eka, clutching Ashwatthama's lost blade, a silhouette of determination amidst the wreckage of their confrontation.

Ashwatthama also sees Yama walking on his bull in the background.

Eka's voice echoes through the cavern, resonating with a mix of triumph and defiance.

Ashwatthama stands frozen, disbelief etched across his features as he struggles to comprehend Eka's unexpected resilience and possession of his cherished sword.

"Where did you find my sword?" Ashwatthama's voice reverberates with a mixture of shock and demand.

"I acquired it from the British after your imprisonment," Eka responds coolly, his tone laced with a hint of amusement.

"You were behind my arrest?" Ashwatthama's accusation hangs in the air.

"In a way, yes. I merely sought to impede your progress, to give myself a chance to pursue you. But in the end, I must admit, I'm rather pleased with the outcome," Eka confesses with a smirk.

"I demand my weapon back!" Ashwatthamma's voice booms with urgency.

"Come and claim it then," Eka retorts, his own voice echoing with a challenge.

Ashwatthama releases several arrows in quick succession, aiming to strike Eka from a distance. However, Eka adeptly intercepts each arrow with his sword, deflecting them effortlessly with precise movements.

Closing the distance between them, Eka advances towards Ashwatthama, his determined stride echoing through the cavern. Sensing the imminent threat, Ashwatthama retreats further into the depths of the cave, wary of confronting Eka while he wields the formidable blade.

As Eka approaches Ashwatthama, he moves cautiously, mindful of the weight and heft of the sword in his grip. The blade, forged from gold and steel, carries substantial weight, and Eka understands that he cannot afford to relinquish his hold on it, as it serves as his sole means of defence.

Ashwatthama, recognising the weight and power of the golden sword in Eka's grasp, hesitates to engage him directly. Despite his agility and speed, he understands the peril of facing Eka head-on while he remains armed with the formidable blade.

With each step deeper into the cave, the only illumination emanates from the bio-luminescent moss, casting an eerie glow that heightens the tension between the two adversaries.

Ashwatthama meticulously plucks the Sanjeevani plants one by one, ensuring Eka doesn't get his hands on them.

"Ashwatthama, you coward! Come and face me!" shouts Eka defiantly into the cavern's depths.

As his challenge echoes through the cave, a fiery arrow streaks towards him. Yet, strangely, the arrow veers off course, missing Eka entirely and igniting the bio luminescent moss instead. The flames consume the moss, casting the cave in a fiery yellow glow, which gradually subsides back to its original green hue.

Caught off guard by the sudden attack on the moss, Eka fails to notice Ashwatthama's swift punch until it's too late. The blow lands squarely, knocking Eka off balance, though he stubbornly clings to the blade in his hand despite the shock. As Ashwatthama swiftly disappears from view, Eka grits his teeth, determined not to relinquish his only defence.

"You think you can defeat me? Resorting to burning plants now, are we?" Eka shouts angrily, his frustration evident in his voice.

They continue to venture deeper into the cave, each step taking them further into the abyss. Ashwatthama is relentless in his mission to eradicate the bio luminescent moss, his determination evident as he ensures to burn away every trace of its glow.

"Where are you hiding, Ashwatthama? Come and face me!" roars Eka, his voice echoing through the dimming cavern.

As the brightness fades, threatening to plunge the cave into darkness, Eka senses Ashwatthama's strategy.

"I know your plan, Ashwatthama. You aim to fight me in the shadows?" Eka's voice reverberates with defiance.

More arrows fly, igniting the bio luminescent moss and casting flickering flames across the cave.

Realising the danger, Eka tightens his grip on the sword, simultaneously rummaging through his bag for something crucial. But his focus on the bag leaves him vulnerable as Ashwatthama silently charges at him, wielding a sharp icicle. The icy weapon grazes Eka's skin, drawing blood, yet he refuses to release his hold on the sword.

"You coward!" Eka's roar reverberates through the cavern, his defiance undiminished even in the face of injury.

As the icicle melts in Ashwatthama's hand, he senses satisfaction at drawing Eka's blood. With a swift motion, he breaks another icicle, preparing to launch another attack on his elusive opponent.

Spotting Eka's silhouette amidst the darkness, Ashwatthama observes his cautious movements from behind a protective rock. Eka strategically positions himself, ensuring he minimises vulnerabilities to attack, choosing a spot between rocks that shields him from assaults on three sides while keeping his back secure against the rock.

Delving into his bag, Eka's hands search for the object he seeks, his attention momentarily diverted from Ashwatthama. Seizing the opportunity, Ashwatthama stealthily advances, icicle in hand, poised to strike. With determined resolve, he charges at Eka, confident that this time, he will force him to relinquish his sword. However, as he moves in for the attack, Ashwatthama is taken aback by Eka's sudden awareness. In a swift motion, Eka readjusts and brandishes his sword towards Ashwatthama, catching him off guard. Despite Ashwatthama's attempt to evade, Eka's blade slices through, severing Ashwatthama's thumb in the process. With a sharp cry of pain, Ashwatthama drops the icicle and hastily retreats, his plan thwarted by Eka's unforeseen resilience.

"Looks like even immortals can bleed," Eka remarks with a smirk, relishing the sight of Ashwatthama's injury.

"How did you see me?" Ashwatthama roars in frustration.

"Technology. I told you, science is evolving, and you have to keep up to date with technology. I'm wearing night vision goggles, and I can see you as clearly as in daylight," Eka explains confidently, gesturing to his gear.

Eka notices Yama, the god of death, riding his bull nearby.

"Even Yama is waiting for you," Eka adds, tauntingly.

Using his acute sense of hearing, Ashwatthama releases an arrow towards Eka. An arrow whizzes past Eka, narrowly missing him.

"Well, Ashwa, the great immortal, is as blind as a bat," Eka continues, his smirk widening.

Ashwatthama decides to venture deeper into the cavern, where even the luminous moss fails to grow. Following the trail of blood left by Ashwatthama, Eka remains determined and follows him.

"You can't hide from me, Ashwatthama. I will follow you even if this cave takes us to Patal," Eka declares, his voice echoing in the cavern's depths.

Curious about Eka's relentless pursuit, Ashwatthama inquires, "How did you find me?"

"Fool! It's technology," Eka retorts angrily. "I tracked you. I told you, science will someday surpass religion. You could have just given me the herb!" he roars, frustration evident in his voice.

Yet another arrow whizzes by, narrowly missing Eka.

"I don't use a phone. How did you track me?" Ashwatthama asks, bewildered by Eka's methods.

"I don't have time to explain science to a layman. Give me the the herb and we will never cross each other's path again!" Eka demands, his voice dripping with impatience.

"I'm leaving the herbs here, but they're worthless now," shouts Ashwatthama. "They've lost their glow, meaning they're no longer potent. I've also made sure to pluck all the Sanjeevani herbs in the cave, so you won't find anything of value here. And mark my words, only one of us is leaving this cave alive," he declares sternly.

In the background, they notice Yama walking on his bull.

"I agree with you. You are not leaving the cave alive, Ashwatthama," Eka declares, his resolve unwavering.

Another arrow whizzes by, narrowly missing Eka as he stands amidst the chaotic scene, his presence a testament to the ongoing battle.

"You're just wasting your arrows. I told you centuries ago to move ahead with science and technology. I can see your arrows coming from a mile," Eka taunts, a smirk dancing on his lips, his confidence apparent even in the face of adversity.

Meanwhile, Ashwatthama assesses his dwindling ammunition, realising he's left with only one arrow. He understands the importance of making every shot count.

Undeterred by Eka's taunts, Ashwatthama presses deeper into the cavern, with Eka shadowing his every move. The unique atmosphere of this particular cavern, marked by an unusual shade of blue moss and clusters of Sanjeevani plants on the cave's roof, hints at the significance of their surroundings.

"Thank you for leading me to a sanctuary of Sanjeevani plants," Eka laughs, his voice echoing through the cavern, momentarily distracted by the sight.

Taking advantage of Eka's distraction, Ashwatthama begins chanting ancient mantras, infusing his final arrow with divine energy. With a determined focus, he releases the arrow, its brilliant blaze blinding Eka and striking the Sanjeevani plants. In horror, Eka quickly discards his night vision goggles and shields himself from the falling icicles as the Sanjeevani plants catch fire, their precious essence consumed by flames. The glasses are shattered by the icicles.

Amidst the chaos, Ashwatthama realizes that his efforts have only resulted in minor injuries to Eka. With no arrows left in his quiver, he reluctantly leaves his bow behind, knowing it's of no use without ammunition. Retreating deeper into the cavern, he aims to regroup and strategise his next move, leaving Eka momentarily disoriented in the aftermath of their skirmish.

Seeking refuge behind a sturdy rock, Eka takes a moment to catch his breath and adjust his vision to the dim surroundings. As he opens his eyes, his gaze falls upon the fallen bow resting on the cave floor. Beside it lie the burnt remnants of the Sanjeevani plants, their charred remains serving as a stark reminder of the relentless conflict that continues to unfold within the cavernous depths.

"Looks like you're left with no weapons," Eka sneers, his voice echoing through the cavern as he observes Ashwatthama's empty hands.

Undeterred, Eka retrieves the fallen bow, his movements deliberate as he cautiously advances deeper into the cave, following Ashwatthama's trail. The darkness envelops him like a suffocating shroud, and his eyes strain to adapt to the absence of light.

"Don't you have any shame, hiding in the darkness?" Eka taunts, his words cutting through the silence like a blade.

"I am not hiding in the dark. This is a sleeping cavern. It's supposed to be like this," Ashwatthama retorts calmly, his voice carrying a hint of defiance.

"I don't care what cavern this is. Come out and face me!" Eka's roar reverberates off the cavern walls, resonating with raw intensity.

"Maintain silence, Eka," Ashwatthama replies, his tone firm and unwavering.

In the midst of the darkness, Eka's keen eyes catch a glimmer of green light amidst the shadows, drawing his attention like a beacon in the night.

"Can you see me now, Eka?" Ashwatthama's voice rings out from the depths of the cave, laced with challenge and anticipation.

Eka's gaze falls upon Ashwatthama, who stands defiantly holding a Sanjeevani plant, the verdant glow illuminating his determined features.

"This is the last plant left, Eka... Do you want it?" Ashwatthama's voice cuts through the darkness, filled with an eerie calmness that belies the tension in the air.

"I need it. Give me the plant, and we can go our separate ways," Eka replies, his tone edged with desperation.

"Silence. This is a holy place," Ashwatthama whispers reverently, a solemnity overtaking his demeanour as he acknowledges the sanctity of their surroundings.

Eka nods in acknowledgment, a glimmer of anticipation flickering in his eyes as Ashwatthama offers a faint smile. With a deliberate motion, he breaks the plant, its ethereal glow slowly diminishing, casting the cave once more into oppressive darkness.

A primal roar shatters the silence as Eka charges toward Ashwatthama, his fury unleashed in a torrent of rage.

"I am going to kill you!" Eka's voice echoes through the cavern, filled with venomous determination.

In the midst of the chaos, amidst the enveloping darkness, Ashwatthama's voice emerges, a mere whisper yet commanding attention.

"Stop shouting, Eka. This is a holy place," he murmurs, his words resonating with a serene assurance that seems to pierce through the cacophony of their conflict.

"Hope it comforts you that you will die in a holy place..." Eka retorts, his voice dripping with sarcasm as the darkness swallows them whole, enveloping them in the eerie tranquillity of the sacred space.

In the suffocating darkness of the cave, Eka's frantic search continues, his sword slicing through the void with ferocious intensity. Amidst the oppressive silence, a voice breaks through, resonating with an eerie plea that pierces the darkness.

"Please, Eka, do not follow me," the voice echoes, each word dripping with urgency and desperation.

"Shut up!" Eka's response reverberates through the cavern, his frustration boiling over into anger as he dismisses the plea with a shout.

Yet, the voice persists, relentless in its repetition, each iteration more haunting than the last.

"Please, Eka, do not follow me," the words echo once more, filling the cavern with an ominous chant that seems to reverberate endlessly.

Driven by a mixture of curiosity and agitation, Eka navigates through the blackness, drawn toward the source of the haunting refrain. As he approaches, he discerns a human-like figure sprawled on the cave floor, the origin of the ceaseless plea.

"Please, Eka, do not follow me," the voice persists, its intensity magnified by the proximity of its source.

In a moment of frenzied desperation, Eka raises his sword high, channeling all his pent-up rage and anguish into a single, savage strike. With a primal scream, he drives the blade downward, plunging it into the figure with a forceful impact that echoes through the cavern, shattering the haunting chorus into a deafening silence.

The man's agonised cries echo through the cavern, interwoven with the persistent repetition of the haunting plea, "Please, Eka, do not follow me," a ceaseless chorus that seems to defy the man's suffering.

As the stabbed man stirs from his unconscious state, Eka's confusion deepens. Though he cannot see clearly in the darkness, he senses the man's imposing stature, towering over even Ashwatthama. Yet, to Eka's bewilderment, the man appears to be coated in a thick layer of bio-luminescent moss, casting an otherworldly glow around him.

With a sudden movement, the man rises to his feet, prompting an unexpected object to tumble from his moss-covered form—an old Nokia phone.

The eerie repetition of Ashwatthama's voice emanates from the device, each recurrence a stark reminder of the enigmatic circumstances unfolding within the cavern.

"What is happening?" Eka's voice reverberates off the walls, laden with frustration and disbelief.

"Thanks to you, I've even picked up some basics of technology. After our last encounter, I acquired this phone," Ashwatthama's voice echoes from the distant reaches of the cave. "You were right; it truly is one of the greatest inventions ever made."

Once again, the recording plays, Ashwatthama's voice echoing through the darkness, taunting Eka with the realisation that even amidst the chaos, his adversary has adapted to the advancements of modern technology.

"Where are you, Ashwatthama? And who is this man I've stabbed?" Eka's demand cuts through the eerie atmosphere, his senses heightened by the unfolding mystery.

As the stabbed man gradually regains consciousness, the cavern becomes a stage for an enigmatic confrontation, shrouded in darkness and uncertainty.

"It's your friend from the stories, King Muchukunda. You have awakened him from his sleep," says Ashwathama, his voice carrying a weight of finality.

Eka's heart sinks as the realisation dawns upon him. He drops his sword, the clang echoing through the cavern. Memories flood back to him, of the tales he shared with the tribals, of the legendary king and his slumber.

As King Muchukunda stirs, a profound sense of dread envelops Eka. He watches in horror as the king's eyes slowly open, emitting an otherworldly glow. A surge of energy courses through Eka's body, causing him to convulse as if caught in the grasp of some unseen force.

In a blinding flash, Eka disintegrates into particles of light, vanishing into the ether. All that remains is a lingering sense of farewell, as Ashwatthama's solemn voice fills the air.

"Travel well, my friend," he murmurs, his words carrying both reverence and sorrow for the fate that has befallen Eka.

□

Chapter 27

Yama

The Present

As Mohan Mahadev descends the tunnel accompanied by his mercenaries, tension hangs heavy in the air.

"This is where we lost the signals," one of the mercenaries reports, his voice echoing off the cavern walls.

Mohan's brow furrows with concern as he instructs his men, "Find him."

The mercenaries fan out, combing through the labyrinthine passages while Mohan follows closely behind, his senses keenly attuned to any sign of their quarry.

After what feels like an eternity, they locate their missing comrades, but there's no trace of Eka.

"We found our men, but no sign of Eka, sir," one of the mercenaries reports somberly, holding out a small terrarium.

Mohan's gaze falls upon the terrarium, recognising the precious cargo it holds. "It's the Sanjeevani plant," he murmurs, his th0oughts racing.

"Keep searching for Eka," Mohan orders resolutely, his voice betraying a sense of urgency. With a determined nod, he takes possession of the terrarium, cradling it protectively as he leads the way out of the cave.

High above, amidst the vast expanse of the sky, Eka finds himself ensnared by the relentless grip of Yama's noose, his body dragged through the celestial realm.

"It is about time I got my noose around you," intones Yama, his voice resonating with the weight of countless destinies. "You escaped me so many times"

As they soar through the heavens, a crackling energy fills the air, heralding the arrival of an impending storm. Suddenly, a blinding bolt of lightning rends the darkness, illuminating the tumultuous sky with its fierce brilliance.

As Eka gazes upon the approaching figure, a profound sense of reverence washes over him. He falls to his knees, a mixture of awe and humility flooding his being. Even Yama, the mighty lord of death, is momentarily stunned by the arrival of the divine presence.

In the distance, amidst the celestial expanse, emerges Lord Shiva, adorned in his resplendent attire that shimmers with divine radiance. His form exudes an aura of unparalleled majesty, commanding the attention of all who behold him. Each step he takes reverberates with the power of creation and destruction, echoing throughout the cosmic realm.

As Lord Shiva draws near, Yama instinctively lowers his head in deference, folding his hands in a gesture of profound respect. In the presence of the divine, even the lord of death acknowledges the supremacy and transcendence of the cosmic order.

Yama's voice reverberates through the celestial expanse as he addresses the divine presence before him. "Greetings, Lord Shiva," he intones with deference.

Shiva regards Yama with a steady gaze, his countenance reflecting a depth of cosmic wisdom. "What are you doing, Yama?" he inquires, his voice carrying the weight of divine authority.

In response, Yama bows his head respectfully before speaking. "I am taking this man to Yamaloka," he explains. "He has led a sinful life, causing pain to his parents, friends, and those around him."

Shiva's gaze softens with compassion as he listens to Yama's words. No, Yama. Eka has earned the merit of Shivaloka on Shivaratri, the holiest of nights," Shiva declares solemnly. "He fasted and participated in the Kotirudra pooja, remaining awake throughout the night. His steadfast devotion, even in the face of adversity, has purified his soul, and all his sins have been washed away by my blessings."

Shiva's words carry the weight of divine authority as he recounts the tale of Eka's unwavering devotion. "Eka demonstrated his commitment to righteousness when he sought refuge in the temple, abstaining from food and water to evade the encroaching threat of Islamic invaders," he explains. "His steadfast resolve and unwavering faith have earned him the grace of absolution."

Yama, acknowledging Shiva's divine decree, releases the noose from around Eka's neck. With a gasp of relief, Eka collapses to his knees at Shiva's feet, overwhelmed by a flood of emotions.

"Forgive me for all the sins I have committed, Lord Shiva," Eka pleads, his voice trembling with remorse. "I will be a loyal servant in your abode."

Moved by Eka's sincerity, Shiva extends his hand, lifting him up with gentle grace. "Rise, my child," he says, his voice resonating with divine compassion. "Your sins are forgiven, and you are welcomed into the fold of divine grace."

With a grateful heart, Eka follows Shiva into the ethereal mist, embarking on a journey guided by divine benevolence and eternal forgiveness.

□

Chapter 28

Bharat 2123 A.D. – Sanatan: Then, Now, Forever...

The Present

In a high-tech lab, doctors work with extreme care, their focus unwavering. Omkar lies peacefully on a bed, surrounded by advanced medical equipment. The doctors carefully extract a liquid from the Sanjeevini plant.

With precision, they inject the liquid into Omkar. Outside the emergency room, Mohan Mahadev watches anxiously through the glass.

One of the doctors steps out.

"Is it done?" Mohan asks, his voice tense.

The doctor nods and gives a thumbs up. A relieved smile spreads across Mohan's face.

As Ashwatthama navigates through the desolate streets, the pervasive aura of destitution hangs heavy in the air. The dilapidated buildings and deserted alleyways paint a bleak picture of poverty and neglect. Yet, undeterred by the grim surroundings, Ashwatthama continues his solitary journey, his unwavering faith in divinity serving as his guiding light.

His path is interrupted by the presence of law enforcement, their authoritative voices breaking the silence of the deserted streets.

"Please leave the area, Sadhu ji," the policeman urges, his tone bearing a mixture of concern and obligation.

Curious about the cause of the commotion, Ashwatthama inquires further, seeking clarity amidst the uncertainty that looms over the neighborhood.

"Why must I leave?" he questions, his voice calm yet resolute.

In response, another policeman steps forward, his words laden with the weight of impending judgment.

"There is a curfew in place, Sadhu ji. The court is set to deliver its verdict today," he explains, revealing the underlying tension that has gripped the community.

"What's the verdict about?" Ashwatthama inquires with genuine curiosity.

"The court is deciding whether this religious place belongs to Hindus or Muslims," the police officer responds solemnly, his words carrying the weight of a deeply divisive issue.

Ashwatthama's expression remains impassive, his inner serenity undisturbed by the turmoil surrounding him. Resolved to uphold his sense of purpose, he finds solace beneath the shadow of the Nandi statue, the ancient guardian of the temple.

Seated in contemplation, Ashwatthama savours the simple pleasures of life, indulging in the ripe fruits that lie before him. His gaze drifts toward the once-majestic temple, now weathered and worn by the passage of time.

Amidst the quiet solitude, Ashwatthama is unexpectedly greeted by the presence of a young man. Startled yet intrigued, he turns to face the newcomer, his eyes widening in astonishment as he beholds the familiar visage of Eka—a figure he believed to have perished before his very eyes.

With a serene smile, Ashwatthama nods and takes a seat beneath the Nandi statue, quietly consuming fruits while casting a sombre gaze upon the once magnificent but now dilapidated temple.

Suddenly, he is interrupted by the unexpected presence of a young man. Startled, he turns to face the newcomer and is astonished to find Eka standing before him, the very same Eka he had witnessed meeting his demise.

"Namaste, Ashwatthama. I was told I would find you here," Eka calmly greets him.

In response, Ashwa's hand instinctively reaches for his sword, his mind racing with questions and uncertainties.

"There's no need for that, sir. I am Omkar, Eka's son. I meant no harm," Omkar reassures Ashwa.

Reluctantly, Ashwatthama sheathes his sword, his suspicions easing slightly at Omkar's explanation.

"How did you know I was Ashwatthama?" Ashwatthama inquires, his curiosity piqued.

Omkar retrieves a collection of old paintings, depicting Ashwatthama and his father, Eka.

"You look the same as you were some 400 years ago," Omkar observes, presenting the aged artworks.

"Guess Eka did find the Sanjeevani," Ashwatthama remarks with a hint of nostalgia.

"And as promised to you, we didn't use it for any other purpose," Omkar affirms, his words carrying the weight of his family's honour.

Ashwatthama nods in acknowledgment but then notices a discrepancy.

"Ashwa, you had the Sanjeevani, but still your hair is turning white?" Omkar queries, his tone laced with concern.

"The world is going to the dogs. There is nothing called right or wrong. Everything nowadays is political correctness," Omkar laments, reflecting on the state of society.

"Why are you here?" Ashwatthama inquires, intrigued by Omkar's unexpected visit.

"I am sure my father is in hell for fighting with you and trying to kill you. I just want you to forgive him so he may have a peaceful afterlife," Omkar explains earnestly, his eyes revealing his inner turmoil.

A warm smile graces Ashwa's lips as he reassures Omkar, "Don't worry, kid. Your father is in Shivaloka. He is very happy there."

"How the hell did he end up there? I was sure he was destined to hell for his misdeeds," Omkar questions, genuinely puzzled by the unexpected turn of events.

"Shiva has his way with the sour ones," Ashwatthama

replies cryptically, hinting at the divine workings beyond mortal comprehension.

"Why would a god want evil ones with him?" Omkar presses further, seeking to understand the enigmatic nature of divine justice.

Imagine two brothers: one virtuous and the other mischievous. Despite occasional good deeds from the mischievous one, society consistently brands him as the "bad child." This perpetual rejection fosters deep resentment and insecurity within him, as he feels society will never afford him a fair chance," explains Ashwatthama.

"Now, consider these brothers as allegories for gods and demons. During the churning of the ocean, both demons and gods toiled equally. Lord Shiva selflessly consumed the poison, purifying the process. However, when it came time for the nectar, only the gods partook, leaving the demons feeling cheated and unjustly treated. In moments of injustice, where does the mischievous child seek solace? Typically, in the unconditional love and acceptance of their parents, who regard both children with equal affection. Similarly, the demons turned to Lord Shiva, confident in his impartiality and commitment to justice. Their unwavering faith and love for Lord Shiva transcended their differences," Ashwatthama explains further, with Omkar listening intently.

"Even the most ruthless individuals would find acceptance and redemption in Lord Shiva's eyes, just as saints would. Eka was not inherently evil; circumstances moulded him. It is heartening to know that he resides in Shivaloka, embraced by the compassionate grace of Lord Shiva," concludes Ashwatthama.

Omkar's voice trembles with emotion as he recounts the legacy of his ancestors. "Dad told me my grandfather started this temple 3,500 years ago—is this true?" he asks, his eyes searching for confirmation in Ashwatthama's expression.

With a solemn nod, Ashwatthama affirms the truth behind Omkar's ancestral lineage, acknowledging the weight of centuries resting upon their shoulders. "Indeed, your family's legacy is woven into the very fabric of this sacred place," he murmurs, his voice carrying the reverence of generations past.

Gazing upon the dilapidated ruins of the once-magnificent temple, Ashwatthama's heart swells with sorrow. "I, too, share your grief at the sight of this once-grand edifice reduced to ruin," he confides, his words heavy with lament for the fading glory of their shared heritage.

Omkar's brow furrows with confusion as he ponders the discrepancy between his family's oral history and the findings of modern archaeology. "I wonder why the archaeological survey's findings said that the temple is only 200 years old," he muses, his voice tinged with disbelief.

A wistful smile plays on Ashwatthama's lips, betraying the weight of untold secrets and the burden of a timeless legacy. "Your father was indeed a great man," he begins, his voice carrying the weight of centuries past. "He didn't orchestrate this meeting by chance. His motives were noble—he sought to ensure that justice prevailed and that the sanctity of our Hindu heritage was preserved," he reveals, his words echoing with the resonance of ancestral wisdom.

Omkar's brow furrows with confusion as he struggles to comprehend the magnitude of his father's actions. However, before he can voice his confusion, Ashwatthama reaches into his bag, his weathered hands retrieving a sacred relic—the original lingam of the temple.

As the ancient artifact is unveiled, a hush falls over the sacred space, the air heavy with the weight of centuries-old secrets. "I found this when your father was vapourised by King Muchukunda," Ashwatthama confides, his voice reverberating with solemn reverence. "I came to return the lingam to its rightful place in this temple. Even King Muchukunda could not destroy this divine artifact," he declares, a flicker of defiance glimmering in his eyes.

Omkar's eyes widen with incredulity as he grapples with the revelation. "But why did my father remove the lingam from the temple?" he questions, his voice tinged with uncertainty.

"He was a visionary," Ashwatthama's voice resonates with reverence as he divulges the hidden truths of the past. "He foresaw the dark clouds gathering over the temples of India, the impending threat to our sacred heritage, and he chose to safeguard the original lingam until the opportune moment," he explains, his words laden with the weight of ancient wisdom.

With a solemn gesture, Ashwatthama entrusts the sacred lingam to Omkar, passing down the legacy of generations past. As Omkar receives the divine artifact into his trembling hands, he is overcome with a profound sense of reverence and responsibility, his heart heavy with the magnitude of the task before him.

"Use your connections, seek out the most formidable legal minds, and entrust them with this sacred relic," Ashwatthama urges, his voice a steadfast beacon of guidance in the face of uncertainty. "They will wield the law as a weapon, ensuring victory in the courtroom and reclaiming the temple for generations to come."

Omkar's eyes blaze with determination as he clutches the sacred lingam close to his heart, a tangible symbol of his unwavering resolve. "I will not falter, I will not rest until justice is served," he vows, his voice echoing with the conviction of a warrior on the brink of battle. "I will win this case for my father, for you, and for all the Hindus of Bharat," he declares, his words a solemn oath etched in the annals of history.

With a solemn yet resolute air, Ashwatthama rises from his seat, his gaze fixed on the horizon of destiny. "Even in his eternal rest, your father continues the sacred battle for Hinduism," he intones, his voice carrying the weight of centuries of struggle. "He was a true guardian of the faith then, he remains so now, and his legacy shall endure for eternity," he declares, his words a solemn tribute to the unwavering devotion of generations past.

Omkar, humbled by the profound gravity of the moment, approaches Ashwatthama and bows before him, seeking his blessings. "Grant me your divine blessings, Maharaj," he implores, his voice reverberating with reverence and determination.

With a gentle yet firm touch, Ashwatthama bestows his blessings upon Omkar, his words echoing with the ancient wisdom of ages past. "May the divine guide your path, may your resolve never waver, and may victory be yours," he intones, his voice a steadfast beacon of hope amidst the tumult of uncertainty.

As they prepare to part ways, Omkar looks to the future with a sense of anticipation. “Until we meet again, in the year 2223, Maharaj?” he asks, his eyes ablaze with determination.

“Yes, in 2223, Omkar,” Ashwatthama affirms, his voice carrying the assurance of a timeless bond that transcends the constraints of mortal existence.

With a final exchange of glances, they bid farewell, their destinies intertwined in the tapestry of time. As they embark on their respective journeys, the echoes of their encounter linger in the air, a testament to the enduring spirit of faith, resilience, and hope that binds them together across the ages.

□□□